THE LADY OF DOOM

Whispers have reached Scotland Yard of an elusive figure that has appeared on the dark horizon of crime and is making its influence felt. Then the first threatening letter comes, demanding a huge payment, or death for its recipient. The victim goes to the police for protection — only to be promptly murdered. The same graft has been worked by gangsters in Chicago — and now it seems they have arrived in London. As Scotland Yard strives to find the criminal mastermind responsible, so too does a mysterious woman . . . the Lady of Doom!

GERALD VERNER

THE LADY OF DOOM

Complete and Unabridged

LINFORD
Leicester

First published in Great Britain

First Linford Edition
published 2017

A catalogue record for this book is available
from the British Library.

ISBN 978–1–4448–3133–7

Published by
F. A. Thorpe (Publishing)
Anstey, Leicestershire

Set by Words & Graphics Ltd.
Anstey, Leicestershire
Printed and bound in Great Britain by
T. J. International Ltd., Padstow, Cornwall

This book is printed on acid-free paper

Prologue

The Killing

Chicago lay beneath a stormy night sky, the blazing lights of its main streets and broad highways shining blearily through the drizzle of rain that had been falling incessantly all day and looked like continuing all night.

The theatres and picture-houses were disgorging their nightly crowds of pleasure-seekers, and the wet pavements and shining roadways were thronged with groups of laughing, chattering men and women, the more fortunate of whom picked their way among the puddles towards waiting cars and taxi-cabs, while the others sought the elevated and the street cars as a means of reaching their homes or in many cases, the dubious entertainment provided by the innumerable dance-places and speak-easies with which the city abounds and from the proceeds of which the liquor

1

kings and gangsters wax rich and fat.

These glittering haunts of iniquity are graded to suit the tastes and pockets of their patrons, and, beginning with the palatial magnificence of the Knickerbocker on Main Street, pass through varying degrees to Eco's near the waterfront. Eco's is neither palatial nor magnificent, and the rye spirit which it serves out to its habitues is raw, cheap stuff, unmatured and in keeping with the general tone of the establishment; for here are to be found no white shirt-fronts and tuxedos, no filmy-clad, bejewelled women such as grace the tables of the more pretentious places.

Eco's does not cater for the upper strata of Chicago's night-life society. At the wooden, plain-topped, drink-stained tables that are scattered thickly over the lino-covered floor can usually be found as mixed a collection of humanity as could possibly be imagined under one roof. Flashily dressed men, typical of the lower classes of hijacker and racketeer, accompanied by equally flashy women, with hard lines about their eyes and mouths that no amount of paint can conceal, congregate to pass on orders from the 'big bosses,' or discuss the latest graft; Chinamen peddling little white packets of 'snow,' one or two blacks, and a sprinkling of the flotsam and jetsam of every nation, constitute Eco's nightly clientele.

Tony Eco himself, the large-faced, greasy proprietor of mixed origin, presides over his establishment from behind the semicircular bar that occupies a corner of the oblong, low-ceilinged room, greeting each fresh arrival with a nod and a smile, and occasionally calling them over to whisper confidentially in their ears as he pours out a tot of the rank poison that is sold under the name of whisky.

On this wet and dreary night, Eco's was even more crowded than usual, and the tall man in the shining, rain-streaming mackintosh who presently pushed open the door and entered, stood for a moment, evidently looking for a vacant table. He was obviously somebody of importance; for the loud chatter of voices became subdued at his appearance, and the fat proprietor himself left the bar and came forward, rubbing his dirty hands ingratiatingly.

'Good evening, Mr. Brandt. Nasty night it is, eh? You want a table?'

Al Brandt nodded curtly, and the stout man shrilled out an order. Two men who had been sitting at a table near the door rose, collected their drinks, and moved over to another table at which a man and a woman were already seated. Tony Eco bowed the newcomer to the vacant place.

'You will drink something?' he asked as the other sat down.

'Brandy,' snapped the man called Brandt. 'And don't try and work off any of that methylated spirit stuff on me.'

Tony Eco raised a hand in protest. 'No, no — the special bottle,' he said. 'I keep always the best for you, Mr. Brandt. I would not dream of giving you anything but the best.'

'You would if you thought you could get away with it, you fat slug,' retorted the other. 'Go on — jump to it. I'm not stopping here all night.'

The proprietor shrugged his shoulders and hurried over to the bar, and Al Brandt, thrusting his hands into his pockets, looked about him, a heavy scowl on his sallow, unpleasant face. His eyes rested for a moment on a tall, slim woman who was standing by the bar talking to an overdressed little man. She nodded, and, saying something to her companion, came over to the table occupied by the new-comer.

'Evenin', Al,' she greeted him pleasantly. 'Seen anything of Mike tonight?'

'I saw him earlier on,' replied Al ungraciously. 'I'm waiting for him now.'

The woman uttered a sigh of relief. 'Oh, well, if he's doing something for you, that's OK,' she said. 'He was going to meet me here an hour ago and I was kinda getting uneasy.'

'I never said he was working for me,' snarled the other. 'I certainly sent him along to Mo's with a message, but that was three hours ago. I expected to find him here with the answer.'

The woman's rather large blue eyes clouded. 'Say, that sets me worrying,' she muttered. 'You don't think anything could have happened to him, do you?'

'How the heck should *I* know what's happened to him?' snapped Al. 'I'm not his keeper. Likely he's run into some dame, and — '

'That's a lie, and you know it!' She swung round on him like a fury. 'Mike Ahearn don't bother with dames. He's not like the rest of your dirty crowd.'

Al Brandt shrugged his thin shoulders. 'A very wifely sentiment, my dear,' he sneered. 'You're not the only Jane who thinks her husband's an angel — until she finds him out. You'll find Mike out one of these days.'

'And what a great kick you'd get if I did, wouldn't you?' she flamed. 'See a possible chance of catching me on the rebound for yourself, eh? Oh, I know the ideas you've got! But you haven't an earthly — not even if Mike turned out the biggest rotter in the world.'

The man's sallow face flushed and his dark eyes blazed. 'See here, Kit,' he hissed, 'you're getting too free with your tongue, and people who start doing that with me get hurt.'

Kathleen 'Kit' Ahearn's lips curled contemptuously. 'I'm not afraid of you, Al,' she retorted, 'not even though you are a pretty big guy. And I know someone else who's not afraid of you either — Lew Gorman.'

Her taunt struck home, and the crimson in Al Brandt's face grew darker and then faded, leaving behind an unpleasant pallor. 'Lew Gorman 'ull be out of business soon,' he snarled. 'There ain't room for two of us working the same graft.'

'Then you'd better look for another,' Kit snapped, 'for it won't be Lew who'll quit.'

'He may not have any choice,' muttered the gang leader thickly. 'He's getting dangerous. Look what happened last week to Dan and Ike — riddled with bullets at the door of the Panther Club. That was Gorman's work.'

'You sure it was Lew's work?' There was a curious note in her voice, and he looked up sharply.

'Sure?' he echoed. 'Of course I'm sure. Who else do you think did it?'

'You've taken great pains to put it around that it was Lew,' she said, ignoring his question, 'but it wasn't Lew sent them to the Panther Club.'

Brandt ripped out an oath. 'What do you mean?' he growled. 'I sent 'em to the Panther Club — '

'Yes,' she interrupted, 'an' somebody was waiting for them to arrive with a machine-gun in a closed car. Did you send that as well?'

Al Brandt started to his feet so suddenly that his chair went over with a crash. 'What the hell are you getting at?' he roared. 'Do you think I put two of my own men on the spot?'

He broke off, interrupted by the hurried opening of the door and the entrance of a wizened, ragged, rain-drenched figure gasping heavily, as though it had been running hard.

'Where's Mrs. Ahearn?' breathed the newcomer with difficulty. 'I've just come from Mo's joint — Mike — '

Kit, her big eyes wide with nameless fear, swung round and gripped him by the arm. 'What's that you're saying, Slim?' she rasped. 'What's that about Mike?'

'Shot,' gasped the little man between his panting breaths. 'Got him — from a closed car as he was going into — Mo's place — '

Kit Ahearn's face went deathly white and in a dazed voice she repeated through scarcely moving lips: 'Mike — shot!'

'Here, Mrs. Ahearn, drink this.' A woman at the next table had risen and was holding out a glass of neat spirit, but Kit pushed it aside. Still clutching Slim by the arm, she turned slowly until she was facing Al Brandt.

'You sent Mike to Mo's three hours ago,' she said between her teeth. 'You sent Dan and Ike to the Panther Club last week.'

Something that he read in her eyes sent a momentary look of fear to his, and she saw it.

'Al Brandt,' she hissed, stepping forward, 'you put Mike on the spot tonight!'

The gang leader passed his tongue across his dry lips. 'You're crazy,' he muttered. 'Clean crazy! Why should I want to put Mike on the spot? He was a good boy, was Mike — one of the best.'

'Why?' she said, still in that same level, monotonous voice. 'I'll tell you why. Mike was getting sick of the game. He was on the point of quitting, and you were afraid that when he did he'd squeal. He wouldn't. He wasn't the squealing sort, but you were afraid. That's one of the reasons. The other is that you've never forgiven Mike for marrying me. You wanted me for yourself.'

'Aw, quit spilling nonsense,' broke in Al Brandt impatiently, but his face was white and strained. 'I tell you you're crazy.'

'Where were you then when Mike was shot?' she flung at him.

'On my way here to meet him,' replied the gang leader. 'See here, Kit, you're all upset. I know nothing about Mike. It must have been Lew Gorman's lot — ' His voice faltered and died away under the cold scrutiny of her eyes.

'I don't believe you,' she said slowly, and the quiet menace in her voice sent an inward shiver through the man who listened. 'But I'll find out for certain, and if you put Mike on the spot tonight, Al Brandt, you can look out for what's coming to you. No matter where you go or where you hide, I'll get you!'

She turned to the wizened, dejected Slim. 'Take me to — to Mike,' she whispered, and, hatless and coatless just as she was, passed out into the streaming night.

A babel of excited voices broke out at her exit, but Al Brandt heard none of the questions that were hurled at him. Tossing down the brandy which the obsequious Tony brought to him, he rose and left the place without a word.

During the walk home to his luxurious flat off Main Street, the hissing of the rain and the soft moan of the rising wind resolved themselves into a whispering voice, the voice of Kit Ahearn repeating over and over again: 'No matter where you go or where you hide, I'll get you!'

END OF PROLOGUE

1

The House by the Crossroads

The characters of houses, like people, differ to a marked degree. Some are cheerful, radiating an atmosphere of cosiness and comfort; others are dour and hard and uninviting. Some are mournful and gloomy, as though brooding over their lost greatness.

Whitegates was such a house as this. It had stood for centuries at a crossroads on the outskirts of Oxshott Common; a low-built, rambling building with unexpected gables and turrets that had, as a matter of fact, been designed by its original owner, a man who knew nothing of architecture but who had allowed his whims and fancies full play.

When he had died, the house had been sold to a retired banker who had added such improvements as he had deemed necessary for his comfort, with the result that the house looked more unprepossessing than before. When in the course of time the banker had followed his predecessor to the grave, the place had passed into the hands of his heirs, and had eventually been put up for sale.

Nobody, however, had appeared eager to buy it, and the agents into whose hands it had been put had long since despaired of ever getting rid of it; indeed, had almost forgotten its existence. The grounds were neglected and choked with weeds and lishy grass that overflowed onto the once well-kept paths like the flooding of a river, and blotted them out of existence. The shrubs and bushes had spread wildly, their long branches trailing over what had once been flowerbeds, gay with colour, but were now a riot of tangled undergrowth and such hardy perennials as had succeeded in fighting the choking weeds and gone on year after year reproducing their own kind.

No one ever came near the old house, and the only sign of life that it had seen for years was the birds that had built their nests in the tall beech trees and the rabbits whose burrows riddled the grass-covered banks. And yet on a certain rainy night, such a night as that on which two years previously Mike Ahearn had been shot down outside Mo's club in Chicago, the dark and silent drive suddenly woke to signs of unusual activity. Out of the black shadows of the night came a muffled figure that slunk in at the broken gate and walked swiftly through the drizzle of rain that was falling, towards the dark entrance of the house. It might have been the very spirit of the place suddenly come to life, for there was nothing to show whether it was man or woman. It moved noiselessly, gliding under the overhanging branches of the trees, and presently disappearing alto-gether as the black bulk of the house swallowed it up.

Once more silence descended on the drear building, and then, after a lapse of time, and at intervals of some two or three minutes' duration, other dim forms began to slink up the old drive; furtive shapes bred of the blackness of the night, evil and unclean. Some were slouching and shabbily dressed, others upright and spruce, but all moved in the same furtive way and all made for the same destination.

In the dark cavern of the bare and dusty hall, the figure who had first arrived stood waiting to receive his strange guests. A weird figure, this person whom they had apparently come to meet. A long black rainproof coat covered him from neck to toe, and in the place where his face should have been was nothing but a black patch.

As each fresh arrival passed him, they muttered a word in greeting and were given a keen scrutiny in the light of the small torch which their silent host held for that purpose. He counted fifteen people in all; and when the last had come and had been ushered into a room on the right, he carefully bolted and chained the front door and joined them.

It was not a pleasant room, and neither was the mixed company it contained. A guttering candle in a bottle supplied the only light. This feeble glimmer was scarcely sufficient to disperse the gloom, but in case any faint ray should percolate to the outside world, sacking had been hung over two large windows. There was a smell of decayed paper, dampness and rotting wood that hung heavily in the air and presently became mingled with that other smell which is generated by damp clothing. The group of men who waited in this room, which may once have been beautiful but was now so ugly, turned and looked at the masked man as he came in and closed the door.

He stood in the shadows so that he was scarcely visible, his face nothing but a patch of blackness caused by the silken covering that concealed it. For perhaps four seconds he stood looking at the faces before him, and then he spoke. His voice was muffled, low and pitched on one note so that even to anyone who was familiar with him it would have been unrecognisable. He spoke rapidly but clearly, and his audience, each of whom he had selected with great care and from various quarters of London, listened, enthralled.

The things he spoke about were strange to English ears, except for certain paragraphs in the newspapers, for the spirit of Chicago had come to that lonely house this rainy November night to lay the foundations of a fresh edifice in the annals of crime. For over an hour he talked, and when he finally concluded there was a murmur of excited comment.

'And you believe that this scheme can be successfully carried out?' asked a thin, gaunt man.

The figure by the window nodded. 'I do,' he answered. 'Provided the lines I have outlined are followed explicitly. As I said before, it has already been entirely successful in America!'

'Well, I'm with you!' said the gaunt man, and the remainder of the assembly expressed approval in their various characteristic manners.

'Then I have only one more thing to say,' went on the masked man, 'and after that we can discuss the final details. The fifteen of you who are here tonight will each be allotted a district, and will be responsible for that district. Once every week we shall meet here, and you will bring me your various reports, and we shall plan fresh campaigns. The date and time of the meetings will reach you the day before, and you will each use the utmost precaution to get to this house without attracting undue attention.'

He took a sheaf of papers from the breast pocket of his long coat. 'Now, I have here a list of the six richest men in the country, together with full details of the amount of their fortunes. You will see that I have marked Abraham Rosenthorne's name with a cross, which means that I propose to start operations with him.'

He moved to the mantelpiece and held the papers under the light of the candle. The others crowded round, and a distant church clock was striking midnight before the strange assembly broke up and by ones and twos, as they had come, left the empty house.

The masked man was the last to leave, and he made his way down the drive a good twenty minutes after all the rest had gone. And yet not quite the last, surely, unless the slim, flitting shape that moved from tree-trunk to tree-trunk was but a figment of the imagination. Whatever it was, it escaped the vigilance of the masked man; and when he squeezed through the half-open gate and disappeared in the darkness of the night, he had no idea that there had been someone else present at that strange gathering — an unseen and unsuspected watcher whose only aim in life was to bring about his death!

2

The Embankment Crime

Detective-Inspector Shadgold looked at the visitor across his big desk with lacklustre eyes. But although his expression was reminiscent of a deceased codfish, it was at these times that the Scotland Yard man's brain was most active.

'When was it you received this letter, Mr. Rosenthorne?' he asked in his ponderous way.

The dark, slightly bald and rather pasty-faced man, whose fat, overdressed body occupied the only other chair in Shadgold's bare and cheerless office, made a typical gesture with his chubby, well-kept hands. 'This morning,' he answered, and there was only the faintest suggestion of the guttural about his voice to point to his un-English origin. 'This morning. By the first post.'

The inspector slowly twisted his bull neck and glanced at the round-faced clock ticking noisily against one wall, saw that the hands pointed to five minutes past ten, and twisted slowly back again. 'At your private house — not at your office, I suppose?' he remarked gruffly.

'At my house in Park Lane,' agreed the other, nodding. 'I do not as a rule reach my office in the City until ten-thirty.'

'I see,' grunted Shadgold. He picked up the sheet of paper that lay on his blotting-pad and read the message it contained for the third time. It was a typed letter, and began abruptly:

'*You are worth two and a quarter million. At how much do you value your life? Dead, your money will be useless to you. To remain alive will cost you a third of your fortune. Bring this amount in bearer bonds to the Thames Embankment at 2 a.m. A man with a sprig of white heather in his coat will meet you by Hungerford Bridge. Do this and continue living — fail and die! This is no idle threat, and you will receive no other warning. Do not attempt to seek help from the police.*'

That was all. There was no date, signature, or anything else.

Shadgold looked at the back of the letter, held it up to the light, put it down, and frowned. 'Maybe it's a joke?' he suggested brightly.

'A choke!' In his excitement the millionaire flung the last remnant of his careful English to the winds. 'Will it be a choke if this threat is carried out?'

Shadgold, looking at him, had his own private opinion about that, but tactfully refrained from putting it into words. Allowing his protruding eyes to wander to the pile of papers beside his blotting-pad, he pursed his lips in thoughtful silence. 'What exactly do you want us to do?' he asked at length, and the millionaire's unhealthy face flushed angrily.

'Surely that is a matter for you to decide,' he said stiffly. 'How can I suggest what you should do? I've come to you for help. I demand protection from these people, whoever they are, and it's your business to see that I get it. Isn't that what the police are for?'

The Scotland Yard man knitted his

brows gloomily. 'I'll look into the matter,' he said, 'though I shouldn't take this letter too seriously if I were you. We get scores of them every day, and mostly they turn out to be somebody's idea of humour or written by a lunatic. This sort of thing doesn't happen in England. Now, if it was America . . . ' He shrugged his shoulders as if nothing that happened in America would ever surprise him.

'But you can't dismiss the thing as lightly as that,' exclaimed the agitated man in front of him. 'Supposing it's not either a joke or written by a lunatic! Am I to be robbed or murdered without any steps being taken to prevent it?'

'No, no, no, certainly not!' broke in Shadgold in a tone that suggested horror at the bare idea. 'Certainly not, Mr. Rosenthorne.'

'Then what do you propose to do?' demanded the outraged man.

'I propose that you keep the appointment at 2 a.m. tomorrow,' answered the inspector. 'I'll arrange to have the place watched, and if anybody comes — well, that will be that. They won't trouble you any more, I can promise you.'

'You will take every possible precaution?' insisted the millionaire. 'I shall be running a tremendous risk.'

'I will attend to all that,' said Shadgold soothingly. 'Now I suggest that you forget all about it until tomorrow.'

After much difficulty, the inspector succeeded in shepherding the uneasy and greatly worried financier out of the office, handed him over to the care of a uniformed constable, and returned to his chair with a sigh of relief.

Mr. Abraham Rosenthorne was in a blue funk, and although the inspector had tried to allay his fears he was by no means certain that they were groundless. Whispers had reached that grim building on the Thames Embankment; ominous whispers of unusual activity in the underworld. London's crook colony that lives in the back streets of Soho and Tottenham Court Road, and farther afield in the purlieus of Deptford and Netting Dale, was in a seething ferment of unrest. Something out of the ordinary was expected.

Certain shabby and shifty-eyed men

who came by night to the little door known as the Traitor's Gate, and earned a dangerous and not very lucrative livelihood by carrying information to the police, had strange tales to tell — vague stories of an elusive figure that had appeared on the dark horizon of crime and was making its influence felt; disquieting stories concerning the sudden appearance of firearms among men who a few weeks before would never have dreamed of carrying a weapon, knowing that to be caught with a pistol meant a heavy addition to their sentence.

Something was brewing, and Shadgold had long been worried as to what it was.

And now had come Rosenthorne and the threatening letter. Was it a joke, or was there a connection? The Scotland Yard man had often expressed a conviction that all the publicity given by the newspapers to the doings of Chicago's gangsters would sooner or later have an adverse effect on criminal London. He had said so again and again. Was his prophecy about to be fulfilled?

There was a very American touch about that letter. The same graft had been

worked in Chicago, and worked successfully. Leaning back in his chair with an
evil-smelling black cigar emitting volumes
of odoriferous smoke, Shadgold remembered a conversation he had had with an
American detective who had come to
London for a holiday.

'If you're a rich man, you've got to pay
to live in Chicago,' his friend had said.
'That's practically what it's come to. The
gangs make you dub up a slice of your
income for the pleasure of being allowed
to spend some of the remainder. And it's
the simplest and most paying graft they've
discovered. Everybody wants to live, and
for every one man who would pay ordinary blackmail, there are a hundred who'll
pay up to avoid being bumped off. You
would yourself.' Shadgold had agreed with
him. Had this menace to civilisation crossed
the Atlantic, and was it the reason for the
systematic arming of the underworld?

Throughout the rest of that day,
Shadgold's mind occupied itself with the
possibilities that his imagination conjured
up. As a matter of routine, he sent the
letter to the fingerprint department, but

the report was negative, and he had expected nothing else.

On the following evening, he made his preparations for the appointment with his usual methodical care, and at the last moment decided to be present in person. He chose three plainclothes men to go with him, and greatly to their surprise supplied each with a fully loaded automatic. 'I've a hunch they may be useful,' he said. 'But don't use 'em unless the other fellow draws first.'

The night was dark, with a chill wind blowing up from the river; and the miserable, huddled-up wrecks of humanity that sprawled on the wide seats lining the Embankment raised pinched, expectant faces as the burly figure of the inspector loomed into view and passed by. Big Ben was striking a quarter to two when Shadgold had finished posting his men and took up his own position by the rising bulk of the bridge, sufficiently far from a light standard to wrap him in gloomy shadow.

A green-lighted police-launch went chugging down river, and behind him an all-night tramcar clanged past, carrying its homeward-bound freight. The scene was prosaic enough, and there was nothing to suggest that it was the setting which fate had selected for the beginning of a reign of terror that was to hold London in its grip for many weeks to come.

Two o'clock boomed out, and the last vibration had scarcely died away when a saloon car came purring along from the direction of Westminster and drew up by the kerb. The stout, flabby figure of Mr. Abraham Rosenthorne got out, and, looking nervously about him, began to walk with lagging steps towards the shadowed base of the bridge. Shadgold, breathing a little faster, watched keenly for the appearance of the man with the white heather, but no such person materialised. The millionaire reached an empty seat and paused irresolutely, gazing to right and left, but the long stretch of the Embankment was deserted save for a crawling taxi that was approaching from Blackfriars.

'Either the man who was to meet him is late, or the letter was a hoax after all,' muttered the Scotland Yard man.

The words had scarcely left his lips

when the crawling taxi slowed and stopped directly opposite the waiting figure of the millionaire. But nobody got out. Instead, there came a sudden staccato rattle, and a pencil of orange flame leaped from the dark interior. Rosenthorne swayed drunkenly, and without a cry, crumpled in a heap onto the seat.

Shadgold sprang to action, the whistle between his lips shrilling out its warning blast, but already the taxi had bounded forward. 'Stop that cab!' he shouted to the three plain-clothes men as they dashed from their places of concealment, but his words were drowned by the harsh clatter of the machine-gun as it opened fire again, and a hail of lead whistled round him.

The sharp cracking of an automatic added to the din as one of the detectives sent a volley in return, but he might as well have tried to hit the wind. It was no ordinary cab engine that beat beneath that battered radiator. The taxi was already gathering speed, and before Shadgold reached the fallen figure of the millionaire its red tail-lamp was vanishing in the distance.

'Is he dead, sir?' panted the man with

the pistol, looking down at the motionless body; and in reply the burly inspector pointed to the six holes in Mr. Rosenthorne's once immaculate shirt-front, now no longer immaculate, but turning rapidly crimson as the blood welled from the wounds.

'Cripes!' muttered the plain-clothes man, his ruddy face the colour of chalk. 'I've never seen anything like it! They meant to make sure.'

'They put him on the spot,' growled Shadgold grimly, and rose to his feet. 'Do you hear that, Bolton? Here in London, they put a man on the spot because he went to the police for protection. It's come at last. I always said it would. Somebody over here has adopted Chicago methods!'

3

Gregory Carr's Decision

The newspapers splashed the killing of Abraham Rosenthorne, giving to the story much space, for the method of the crime was a novelty in England. Criminologists wrote long articles about the Chicago menace, and the general public read both news and articles with gusto, and smiled. They smiled less and less during the ensuing weeks, and with reason, for a wave of crime of a new kind began to engulf London and strike terror into the hearts of the citizens.

Close on the heels of the murder of Rosenthorne came the hold-up of the Consolidated Bank. Shortly after the bank opened its doors, three cars filled with men drew up outside. While half their number guarded each side of the entrance with machine-guns, the remainder entered the building, holding up the staff at the point of automatics, and clearing out something in the region of one hundred thousand pounds which had arrived on the previous day from the Bank of England for a special payment concerning a government loan. Two bank clerks were seriously wounded, and three policemen shot dead, but the gangsters involved got away.

Within a week four more outrages of a similar nature had occurred, and the police were helpless to cope with the new menace; for what use is a rubber truncheon against more deadly weapons? The Metropolitan Constabulary were not allowed to carry firearms.

Something like a panic began to spread rapidly, for many rich men had received similar letters to that which the dead Rosenthorne had taken to Scotland Yard. Richard Harrage, the steel king, found one waiting on his breakfast-table, and, remembering the fate of Rosenthorne, paid up the demand, and lived.

Mr. Joshua Salmon, whose string of picture-theatres extended almost from Land's End to John o' Groats, also paid. Alexander O. Willis openly defied the demand, and in consequence provided a full page in the Sunday papers. He was shot dead outside the drive gates of his house at Esher one Saturday morning, and the doctors who examined him counted nine bullet-wounds in his body from the automatic that had killed him.

Following this tragedy, many men must have paid in silence, fearful of the results of consulting the police, for no reports reached either Scotland Yard or the press.

That celebrated dramatist, Mr. Trevor Lowe, read the newspaper accounts of the tragedies, and was interested. But it was not until Gregory Garr got mixed up in the business that he took any active part in the gang menace that so suddenly burst upon London; and then his interference in the matter was the result of pure accident.

After the killing of Willis, there was a lull in the gang's activities, and it was during this period of quiescence that Gregory Carr, seated in his small bachelor flat overlooking the Green Park, came to the conclusion that it was necessary to make drastic alterations with regard to his finances. The morning's post, which had consisted of a large number of peremptory letters demanding money, and a later visit to an adamant and inclined-to-be-offensive bank manager, had combined to bring about this state of mind.

Something had got to be done. An inspection of his entire wealth had brought to light three pound notes, eighteen-and-sixpence in silver — and four pence! Not very helpful when one considered that the rent of the flat was two quarters overdue and the agents were threatening proceedings, and that the rest of his debts ran into four figures.

Gregory rose, lighted a cigarette and stared gloomily out at the streams of traffic and people hurrying along Piccadilly. What a fool he had been to invest all his modest capital in that company of Rosenthorne's. But then, who could have foreseen that the man would be killed? His death, of course, had sent the shares toppling to nothing. Gregory ground his teeth. Confound the gangsters who had shot him!

He crushed out the stub of his cigarette, lit another, and for the hundredth time surveyed his position from all angles. He would have to give up the flat, that was certain; his car had already gone, and so had everything else that he possessed of any value, except that. But it was more of a liability than an asset. He had been trying to sell the dilapidated old house at Oxshott for years, but nobody seemed to want it. It was too large to dispose of easily, and in the wrong position for the site to be of any value for building purposes. It was also badly in need of repair; everything that was possible to leak leaked, and that was over four years ago. He hadn't seen it since then. What it was like now, heaven knew!

Still — a sudden thought struck him — if it couldn't be sold, it might yet be made to serve a useful purpose. If he was forced to give up his flat, he would have to live somewhere, and perhaps there were at least a couple of rooms at Whitegates that could be made habitable. One advantage was that there would be no rent to pay, and it would give him time to look round for a job.

Gregory nodded to himself. Yes, it was an idea. He would go down and have a look at the place. At any rate, it was better than sticking indoors and brooding over his troubles. He filled his case with cigarettes, found an electric torch in his bedroom — for it would be dusk by the time he got there — and, struggling into his overcoat, set off on his expedition.

The crossroads near which the house was sited was nearly two miles from Oxshott station, and by the time Gregory arrived at the broken drive gate it was quite dark. As he looked up the gloomy, weed-covered drive that led to the house, he cursed himself for not having put off his voyage of exploration until the following morning. The delay in getting the key from his solicitor had made him later than he thought. However, he was here, and he decided that he might as well have a look over the place. The torch he had brought with him was a pretty strong one, and so he ought to have sufficient light for his purpose.

The gate, he found, was firmly embedded in the gravel and would not move one way or the other, but there was enough room between it and the post to squeeze through, and he began to walk up the tree-shaded drive. His spirits, which had brightened somewhat at the start of his journey, sank almost below zero at the evidence of desolation that surrounded him on all sides. Even if part of the place proved habitable, he shuddered at the prospect of living there. It would be enough to drive anyone to suicide. Still, if the worst came to the worst, it would be better than the Embankment, and that was the immediate prospect that threatened him.

A turn in the winding path brought him in sight of the house — a grim, weather-beaten pile of crumbling brick, silent and forbidding. The dark bulk of it frowned ominously and a muttered sinister warning was in the eerie rustle of the ivy in the night breeze. The broken porch, a darker patch of shadow against the black of the building, gaped like an open mouth.

Ascending the cracked steps towards this unprepossessing entrance, Gregory felt in his pocket for the key. His fingers had closed round it when his eyes, growing accustomed to the gloom, showed him that the heavy door was already half open! He frowned, and a slightly unpleasant sensation prickled the hairs on his neck. Why was the front door of this deserted mansion open? An explanation occurred to him even as the question entered his mind. Of course — it was sheer carelessness on the part of his solicitors. They must have been showing somebody over the place and forgotten to lock up afterward. He would probably find the place being used as a free lodging-house for all the vagrants in the neighbourhood.

Pulling his torch from his pocket, he pushed the door open wider and stepped into the darkness of the hall beyond. His finger was on the button when a blinding ray of light flashed in his eyes and a muffled exclamation made him start. Before he could move, he was gripped roughly by the arm, and a cold circle of steel pressed firmly against his throat.

'I don't know who you are or what you're doing here, my friend,' growled a low, menacing voice, 'but you don't leave this place alive!'

4

Taken for a Ride

For a moment, utter astonishment robbed Gregory of the power of speech and action. Then, as he recovered from the first shock of surprise, he tried to wrench himself free from the vice-like grip on his arm.

The muzzle of the pistol was pressed deeper into his flesh. 'I shouldn't advise you to do that,' warned the man who held him. 'If you struggle I shan't hesitate to shoot, and the position of this gun makes it impossible for me to miss.'

Gregory kept still. There was something in the tone of the other's voice that convinced him that the threat was not an idle one. 'What the deuce is the idea?' he demanded angrily.

'That's what I want to know,' answered the unknown. 'What are you doing spying round this house?'

'Well, I like that!' exclaimed Gregory, his rising anger overcoming his first momentary alarm. 'Seeing that it belongs to me, I've a perfect right to come and look at it if I want to. Who the dickens are you, and what are you doing here?'

He felt the other's start of surprise. 'Belongs to you, does it?' said his captor, ignoring the question. 'Do you mean that you're the owner of this house?'

'That's what I said,' replied Gregory. 'I'd no idea, though, that I had a tenant.'

'Then you're not a detective?' snapped the man in the dark.

'A detective? Good God, no!' said Gregory. 'Look here, what's the joke? I come down to look over my own property, and get a gun jabbed in my throat.'

'There is no joke,' snarled the other grimly. 'It's a pity for your sake that you didn't keep away or choose the day-time for your visit.' He swung Gregory round, without, however, shifting that menacing circle from its position against his neck. 'March!' he ordered briefly.

For a second Gregory was tempted to tell him to go to blazes and take the consequences, but a warning movement of the pistol decided him. Discretion, in this case, was the better part of valour, and he marched.

He was guided towards a door on the right of the big bare hall, which he knew led into a room that had at the time of the house's prosperity been the dining room. The man at his side kicked sharply on the panelling, there was the rasp of a key, and the door was opened from within. A feeble glimmer of yellow light fanned out into the darkness, and the man who held Gregory propelled him into the room. Half a dozen men were standing by the fireplace and he saw that the light came from two candles that had been stuck on the mantelshelf. There was a swelling murmur of alarm as they caught sight of Gregory, which was instantly checked by his captor.

'Stop that noise,' he snarled, and the muffled tone of his voice which had rather puzzled Gregory was accounted for by the fact that he wore a black silk hood that covered face and chin. 'Here, Joe, go out into the hall and wait for Cornish.

41

After he's come, you can bolt and chain the front door and come back here.'

A small, wizened, cross-eyed man detached himself from the group and shuffled forward. 'Who's this guy?' he asked, jerking his head at Gregory.

'I don't know,' snapped the masked man. 'He says that he's the owner of this place, but we've got to make sure of that. Whoever he is, he knows too much to be allowed to get away. Run the rule over him, Lurgon.' He released his hold of Gregory's arm and gave him a push that sent him staggering into the middle of the room.

With a sudden rush of rage that made the veins in his temples swell dangerously, Gregory swung round on the burly figure that approached him.

'You keep your filthy paws to yourself!' he roared. 'I don't know what sink of iniquity I've stumbled into, but I'm — '

'You're going to keep quiet unless you want a bullet in you,' hissed the man who was evidently the leader of the outfit. 'And I'm not talking because I like the sound of my own voice. If you've got any doubts about it, just remember what happened to Rosenthorne and Willis and alter your opinion!'

Rosenthorne and Willis! The truth burst upon Gregory like a thunder-clap. By accident he had fallen into the clutches of the gang who were terrorising London. This empty and deserted house of his had been the place chosen for their headquarters! He was so dazed by the discovery that he allowed the unpleasant-looking man with the scar across his chin to unbutton his coat and run through his pockets without remonstrance.

The masked man, who was still covering him with the automatic, chuckled. 'I'm glad you realise now that this isn't a joke,' he sneered, and came over to the little heap on the floor that had been disgorged from Gregory's pockets. The key of the house had a label attached to it, and this he glanced at and dropped into his own pocket, turning his attention to Gregory's anything-but-bulky wallet. Contemptuously ignoring the few notes it contained, he drew out eight or nine visiting cards and scrutinised the name and address.

'It seems as if you were speaking the truth,' he remarked, keeping the card and tossing the pocket-book back behind him with the keys that formed the remainder of the collection. 'Now the question is, what are we going to do with you?'

Gregory kept silent, his brain working busily to try and find some way out of this unpleasant situation. He could expect no quarter. Human life meant nothing at all to these people. To make a dash for it would be suicidal. The odds were eight to one, and the one wasn't even armed. He had unwittingly walked into a hornets' nest, and it looked as though he was going to get badly stung.

The voice of the masked man speaking again jarred in on his thoughts. 'I don't want any killing here,' he said. 'You can drive a car, can't you, Lurgon?' The scarred man who had turned out Gregory's pockets nodded. 'Well, then, take this fellow for a ride, run him out into the country, and leave him somewhere at the side of the road after you've made sure that he won't be in a position to open his mouth about what he's seen tonight.'

'That's a good idea,' grunted the gangster.

'All my ideas are good ones,' retorted the other coolly. 'You'd better take Merlin with you. My car's hidden in a field about fifty yards beyond the gate. Now go along and get it over. There's a lot of other things to be attended to and it's getting late.'

'Come along, you,' growled the man who had been appointed executioner, gripping Gregory's arm. 'And don't try any tricks, or you won't get as far as the country.' He accentuated his words with a heavy automatic.

Gregory felt an almost irresistible desire to smash his clenched fist into that leering face and hang the consequences, but he refrained. The time to put up a fight would be when he had only two of them to tackle. Therefore, he permitted himself to be led to the door like a lamb, though his heart was seething with rage, and he made a mental vow that if he did succeed in escaping with his life he would spend the rest of it getting his own back on all of them.

Joe was still lurking in the hall waiting for the unpunctual Cornish, and the man called Merlin who had taken Gregory's other arm held a brief whispered conversation with him before they went out into the darkness.

Telling him the joyful news, I suppose, thought Gregory grimly. *Well, it certainly looks as if I've found a way of dodging my creditors, anyhow.*

Any hope he had of making a dash for it after leaving the house was quickly shattered, for the scarred man rammed the gun barrel into his ribs.

The car, which had been driven into a natural screen of bushes, proved to be an open tourer with a long, lean radiator that spelled speed. Gregory was shoved into the back seat, and Merlin took his place beside him, the other gangster climbing up behind the wheel. It took a little manoeuvring to get the car out of the field, but the driver succeeded at last and sent it hurtling along the straight hedge-lined road that led northwards.

Merlin was evidently taking no chances, for he kept a tight grip of Gregory's arm, and the pistol in his other hand never wavered. On through the darkness raced the car, and with each rhythmic throb of the powerful engine Gregory's heart sank lower. All chance of escape seemed hopeless. Not for a single instant did the man at his side relax his vigilance, and the road was running through a stretch of open country. At any moment the gangster might decide upon a suitable spot. Feverishly Gregory flogged his brain for a feasible plan to save himself, and then Merlin pronounced his doom. Without shifting his position, he shouted to the man in the front seat: 'There's a turning about half a mile ahead that'll be OK. Pull up there, Lurgon.'

The driver nodded to show that he had heard, and the pace of the car increased. So this was the end, thought Gregory. Well, at least he'd make a fight for it, and he was just bracing himself for an attack on his guard when without warning a big laden motor-lorry swung out of a concealed turning almost under their radiator.

Lurgon swerved sharply to avoid a collision, and the resultant jerk sent

Merlin sprawling away from Gregory into the opposite corner of the seat. For a fraction of a second, the gun he held was twisted away from his prisoner, and in that second Gregory acted. Before the gangster had time to recover, he flung himself upon him. Gripping the hand that held the pistol, he forced his knee into his chest and pinned him back against the cushions. Merlin shouted loudly to the man at the wheel, and Lurgon half-turned to see what was happening. His head was halfway round when Merlin's elbow came in violent contact with the hard wooden top of the door, and involuntarily his fingers squeezed on the trigger of the automatic he still held.

There was a sharp report and Lurgon slumped forward over the wheel, the bullet drilling a neat hole through his left temple. His arm caught in the throttle lever as he slithered sideways and jerked it round. The car gave a leap forward, swung out of its course, and headed straight for a tall hedge at the side of the road. Crashing through, it wobbled erratically a few yards into the ploughed field beyond, struck a mound of earth and overturned, shooting Gregory and the still-struggling Merlin out as it did so. They described a beautiful arc and landed with a thud that knocked what little breath Gregory had left out of his body. He felt a sharp pain stab through his head, and then the night became very dark indeed.

5

The Silence of Merlin

Gregory's senses came back to him to the accompaniment of three separate and distinct sensations — a splitting pain in his head, a flood of unprintable language in his ears, and the rather pleasant smell of a distinctive and elusive perfume. Puzzled by the last, he opened his eyes. A slim figure was kneeling by his side, and the scent evidently came from a wisp of handkerchief which was being used to wipe his forehead.

'Oh, you're better — I'm so glad,' said a soft voice. 'I was getting frightened.'

Gregory liked the voice. He had read in books of voices that their authors had described as musical, but until now he had always considered this an exaggeration. He tried to see more of the owner of that voice and succeeded in catching a shadowy glimpse of a small shapely head and a close-fitting red hat.

A further string of imprecations from near at hand turned his attention from this pleasant vision, and he strove to discover from whence they came.

'It's — it's — that awful man,' said the woman in the red hat. 'Isn't it dreadful? I've tied him up.'

Gregory looked into a pair of wide eyes with astonishment. 'Oh,' he murmured, 'you've — er — tied him up, have you?' He scrambled to his feet, wincing as the movement sent a knife-thrust through his head, and went over and looked down at the gangster Merlin. His hands and feet had been skilfully tied with his own necktie and handkerchief.

'You were both unconscious when I found you,' explained the woman, 'so I thought I'd better make certain that he wouldn't get away.'

'You've done excellently well,' said Gregory; and then, looking round: 'What about the other — er — gentleman?'

He sensed rather than saw the shiver she gave. 'He's dead,' she replied in a low voice.

Gregory searched in his pockets for a cigarette, remembered that all his possessions had been taken from him at Whitegates, and shrugged his shoulders in resignation.

'Is this what you want?' The red-hatted lady was holding out a small gold case which she had taken from her handbag.

'You're an amazing person,' remarked Gregory as he helped himself to one of the cylinders of tobacco. 'How did you happen to turn up here so opportunely?'

'I followed you from the house,' she said calmly, and he nearly dropped his cigarette in his surprise.

'You followed me from the house?' he repeated slowly. 'Do you mean to say you were there?' She nodded. 'What in the world were you doing there?' he demanded.

'Watching,' she answered shortly.

'Why?' His voice was incredulous. This was indeed a night of surprises.

'That,' she replied curtly, 'is no concern of yours. You ought to be thanking your lucky stars that you're alive instead of asking questions.'

Gregory felt himself flushing at the

snub, but before he could speak she went on rapidly: 'And now the best thing you can do is to get away from here as soon as possible.'

'But what about this fellow?' He jerked his head towards the helpless gangster who was glaring at him with hate-filled eyes. 'What are we going to do with him?'

She made an impatient movement. 'You can do what you like with him,' she said, 'now that you've recovered. I'm not going to stay here any longer, and I advise you not to remain too long.' She moved away, but Gregory went after her.

'Here!' he protested. 'You can't go like that!'

'That's where you're mistaken,' she retorted coolly. 'I can, and I am, going — just like that. Goodbye!'

She walked rapidly away, and was lost in the gloom before he could think of a feasible method of detaining her. He heard the soft purr of a starting engine and the dwindling whine of a car as it faded in the distance.

With his mind a chaotic whirl of disjointed thoughts, Gregory lighted his

cigarette and, inhaling the smoke gratefully, tried to decide what he should do
next.

* * *

The sergeant in charge of the little police
station listened stolidly to Gregory's story,
wrote it all down carefully and laboriously, and, having secured his signature,
ordered the still-dazed and cursing gangster to be locked up.

Gregory had come to the conclusion
halfway through his cigarette that the best
course he could pursue was to shepherd
Merlin to the nearest police station and
hand him over. He had carried this out,
gaining no little satisfaction from the pleasure of ramming Merlin's own automatic
into that fluent gentleman's ribs during
the journey.

The search for the police station had
not proved difficult, for less than a hundred yards from the scene of the wrecked
car he had come upon a patrolling policeman. This officer, after he had recovered
from his initial amazement, had taken them

both under his wing and marched them to their destination. It was a noteworthy fact that Gregory carefully suppressed all mention of the woman in the red hat when he told his story.

'I'm afraid I shall have to detain you, Mr. Carr,' said the desk sergeant ponderously after a lengthy telephone conversation with Scotland Yard. 'Inspector Shadgold, who is in charge of this gang business, is coming here at once, and would like to have your statement at first hand.'

Gregory had no objection to this arrangement. In fact, he rather welcomed it, for there was no means of getting back to his flat that night unless he walked, and he certainly didn't like that idea. So, making himself comfortable before the fire in the charge-room, he whiled away the time chatting to the station sergeant.

Shadgold arrived about two hours later in a rakish-looking police car, accompanied by a pleasant-faced man with smiling grey eyes whose appearance struck Gregory as vaguely familiar. Recognition came to him in a sudden flash of memory, and as the Scotland Yard man went over to the desk and spoke to the sergeant in charge he sprang to his feet.

'Lowe, by Jove!' he exclaimed with a note of surprised pleasure in his voice. 'I haven't seen you for ages.'

'How are you, Carr?' The dramatist gripped the outstretched hand and shook it warmly. 'Must be at least two years since we met. At Ashcroft's shooting-box, wasn't it?'

Gregory nodded. 'Yes,' he said. 'I've often been going to look you up, but I've kept putting it off, and now — '

'And now we've met again quite accidentally,' broke in Trevor Lowe. 'I happened to be talking to Shadgold of the Yard when the message came through. I came along with him out of sheer curiosity; I'd no idea that you were the Carr involved in this business.'

'You know each other?' Shadgold had joined them. 'Good! Sorry to have kept you hanging about, Mr. Carr, but we called at your place at Oxshott on the way. 'Fraid the birds had flown, though. I've left my men in charge, in case any of the gang should come back. Not that it's likely. They'll know by now that you're still alive, and they'll keep clear of the place.'

'How will they know?' asked Gregory in surprise, and the Scotland Yard man grinned.

'News travels quickly among the criminal classes,' he replied. 'I'll bet they had somebody watching and saw us arrive. When those two fellows who took you for a ride don't go back, they'll put two and two together.' He sat down and became suddenly official. 'Let's hear the story,' he said.

Gregory told them, and both Lowe and the inspector listened intently. He again refrained, however, from mentioning the woman.

'You must have been born lucky, Mr. Carr,' commented Shadgold. 'And it's better to be born lucky than rich, they say. I wasn't born either, so I can't say.'

'Was there a woman among the gang?' asked Trevor Lowe, breaking the brief silence that followed, and Gregory started.

'I never saw one,' he answered.

Shadgold looked at his friend curiously.

'What's the idea, Mr. Lowe?' he enquired.

'No idea at all, Shadgold,' replied the dramatist. 'Only, there was a woman in that house, and if she wasn't with the gang I should very much like to know what she was doing there.'

'How do you know there was a woman there?' demanded the Scotland Yard man.

Lowe smiled and put his hand into his pocket. 'Because I found this upstairs on the first landing,' he replied, and held out a small square of lace-edged cambric.

A faint, elusive perfume reached Gregory's nostrils, and there was no need for him to worry his memory as to where he had smelt it before. It was the same as that used by the woman in the red hat whom he had found bending over him when he recovered consciousness.

Trevor Lowe saw the faint start he gave, and wondered at its cause, but said nothing. 'If you look at the top left-hand corner, you will see that whoever this handkerchief belonged to bore the initials A.C.,' he continued.

The inspector bent forward and peered at the monogram. 'Humph!' he grunted.

'It's strange. It's an expensive handkerchief, too. They must have a woman working with them, then. Perhaps that gangster — what's his name, Merlin? — can tell us something about her. We'll have him on the carpet.' He swung round. 'Fetch that fellow up here,' he called to the station sergeant, and that worthy nodded and disappeared through a door at the back of the charge room.

'If I can only make him talk,' growled Shadgold, 'he may be able to give us a line to the rest of the bunch. I shall sleep sounder when they're all put away. Whoever the fellow is at the head of the outfit, he's a clever guy.' There was a grudging note of admiration in his voice. 'A very clever guy! He's got the brains. He knows that the average English crook's just a cheapskate who hates firearms and 'ud rather go down for a fifteen stretch than use 'em. It's dope and bad liquor that makes 'em so brave in Chicago, an' so he's been distributing snow wholesale. These half-wits 'ull try anything they get for nothing, and once they're all lit up they don't care if they kill a regiment.'

'So that's it, is it?' remarked Trevor Lowe. 'I wondered what was at the bottom of these gang-crimes. Have you any idea who it is who's giving away this free cocaine?'

Shadgold shook his head. 'No; I wish I had,' he said. 'My theory is that it's an American gangster who has made Chicago too hot to hold him, and set up business over here. There's an American touch about the whole thing. It was just before the killing of Rosenthorne that this epidemic of drug-taking broke out in the underworld. We've pulled in a dozen or more little sneak thieves and smash-and-grab men all suffering from dope, and the meekest of 'em was murder-mad until the drug wore off. There's no mistake that that's what's at the bottom of this outbreak — '

He stopped as a constable and the desk sergeant returned, escorting a bruised and sullen-faced Merlin between them. The gangster scowled at Lowe and Gregory, and then stood eyeing Shadgold in silence.

'Well, what have you got to say for yourself?' demanded the Scotland Yard man gruffly.

'Nuthin'!' came the ungracious reply.

The burly inspector's bushy eyebrows contracted ferociously. 'Nothing, eh?' he snapped. 'Your name's Merlin, isn't it?'

A sullen nod was the only answer.

'Lost your tongue, have you?' Shadgold pulled at his moustache. 'Well, we'll have to help you find it. What have you charged this fellow with?' He shot the question at the desk sergeant.

'Attempted murder,' answered that worthy.

'Charge him with murder,' grunted the inspector briefly. 'Wilful murder by shooting a man called Lurgon through the head.'

A look of alarm crossed Merlin's battered face, and his eyes shifted uneasily. 'That's a bloody lie, mister!' he cried. 'I never shot him. That gun went off accidental. This chap 'ere can prove that.' He appealed to Gregory.

'He can't prove anything of the sort,' said Shadgold quickly before Gregory could open his mouth. 'But I might be inclined to believe you — under certain circumstances. You belong to this gang of cut-throats who've been so busy lately, don't you? Who's your boss?'

The gangster's face set stubbornly, and after waiting for a short interval and getting no reply, Shadgold repeated his question.

'Yer wastin' yer breath. I ain't squealin',' muttered Merlin.

'Do you know?' broke in Lowe quickly.

'No. And if I did, it wouldn't make no difference,' said the gangster doggedly. 'I ain't squealin'.'

'You're a fool!' snapped Shadgold angrily. 'Take him back to the cooler, Sergeant, and alter that charge to murder. We'll see if he comes to his senses in the dock!'

Merlin's heavy face went grey. 'I don't know who the boss is, s'elp me, I don't!' he protested huskily. 'But if yer'll stop that charge, I can tell yer something that might help yer.'

'Come to your senses, have you?' growled the Scotland Yard man. 'All right, my lad, fire away.'

'There's a place near — ' began the gangster, and stopped suddenly, his jaw dropping and his eyes bulging in terror. He was gazing in the direction of the door, and Trevor Lowe spun round. He caught a momentary glimpse of a masked figure that filled the entrance, and then there was a dull *plop* from the long-barrelled gun it held. With a little choking cough, Merlin sagged at the knees and collapsed on the floor.

The dramatist sprang forward, but a second bullet scored a crimson slash across the back of his hand. Shadgold and Gregory stood paralysed with amazement, and before Lowe could make any further move the killer had swung round and dashed out of the doorway.

'After him!' exclaimed Trevor Lowe, and ran to the door. But by the time he reached the top of the steps, the masked man had vanished. He heard the throb-throb of a retreating car, and, looking in the direction of the sound, made out a red tail-light disappearing in the distance. In a trice he was across the strip of pavement and at the wheel of the police car, but it hadn't moved two yards before he discovered that the tyres were flat.

A sadder and wiser man, he came back to find Shadgold and Gregory bending over the unconscious figure of the policeman who had been on duty at the entrance to the station. 'Coshed!' exclaimed the inspector, and twisted round to the horrified sergeant. 'Phone all stations to stop a closed car making towards London!' he snapped.

'You won't catch them,' said Lowe decidedly. 'They'll turn off the main road for sure. Let's go and look at that poor fellow Merlin.'

He re-entered the little station, coughing as the acrid fumes of cordite that still filled the charge room caught him by the throat. Kneeling beside the sprawling figure in the centre of the room, he looked at the spreading stain that was soaking into the bare boards.

'Clean through his head,' he commented. 'Poor devil! He was right. There's no squeal coming from him.'

6

The Warning

Where Vauxhall merges into Battersea, there is a semicircular stretch of road that follows the winding course of the river. It is anything but a pleasant locality, for although the street cars jangle their way along its narrow confines, it is at night ill-lighted and at all times squalid and evil-smelling. On either side it is bounded for the most part by a high brick wall intersected every so often by the wooden gates giving admittance to wharf or warehouse; and above these dingy barricades can be seen the tall bulk of ungainly buildings, the skeleton ironwork of cranes or the slender soot-crusted clusters of factory chimneys. Although so unprepossessing to the eyes, it is the centre of honest work where men toil with their hands from early morning till late at night in the granaries and breweries and at other forms of employment which find a home in the ramshackle buildings lining the water's edge.

The first grey streaks of the coming dawn were beginning to silhouette the chimneys blackly against the lightening sky when a car thundered down the narrow roadway and stopped with a jerk outside a closed gate that bore the inscription 'Bell's Wharf' in nearly obliterated letters.

Two men got out, one of whom, producing keys, fumbled with the padlock fastening of the wooden gate. Pulling up the rusty iron bar, he swung the barrier open, and a third man, who was seated at the wheel of the car, drove it into the littered yard beyond. The other two followed, closing the gate behind them, and, being joined by the man in the car, proceeded to pick their way among the rubbish to a small door that was set in the right hand corner of the yard. This was also opened by the man with the keys, and all three passed inside.

The door opened into a narrow passage, pitch-dark and musty-smelling. They had scarcely crossed the threshold when, heralded by a sharp click, a feeble yellow light sprang to life from a dirty electric globe suspended from the ceiling. The passage ended in a big, bare, empty room, about the walls of which stood broken packing-cases from which mildewed straw overflowed on to the rotting floor.

The three men who had come to this dismal-looking place at such an early hour seemed thoroughly familiar with their surroundings, for without pause they crossed the wide expanse of flooring and halted in a corner on the opposite side. The man with the keys stooped and rapped sharply on the boards beneath his feet. There was a momentary silence while they waited. Then came the muffled grinding of a rusty bolt, and an irregular portion of the floor dropped like a trap, disclosing a flight of steps leading downwards, and the head and shoulders of a fourth man.

'The boss is waitin' for you,' he growled as the other three began to descend. 'Did yer manage it?'

The man who had knocked nodded. 'Yes,' he replied, 'and we were only just in time, too. 'E was on the point of squealing.'

The other grunted. 'Bit of bad luck last night altogether,' he said. 'The boss ain't 'alf wild about it, neither. Come on, it won't make 'im any better if he's kept waitin'. 'E wants ter get away.'

The steps ended in a brick cellar, and after he had closed and rebolted the trap, the man who had let the others in crossed to a heavy door at the end and pushed it open. 'They've arrived, guv'nor,' he announced.

The masked man who had been seated at the plain deal-topped table in the square, cell-like room beyond rose to his feet. 'Well,' he said harshly, 'did you settle with Merlin?'

'Yes,' said the spokesman of the trio. 'He won't be able to say nuthin' no more.' He gave a brief account of the shooting of the gangster.

'Just going to squeal, was he?' murmured the man in the mask. 'I always thought Merlin was a squeaker.'

'He won't squeak anymore,' was the brutal reply.

The masked man tapped the table-top thoughtfully. 'What about the other fellow who came to the empty house?'

'I couldn't do anything with him,' replied the gangster. 'It wasn't my fault,' he added hastily, as the masked man muttered something impatiently. 'I only had a chance of two shots before the gun jammed.'

The tall man behind the table leaned forward. 'He's got to be disposed of,' he snarled. 'That man is dangerous. He's in a position to recognise most of us, and don't forget it. You must go out after him at once without delay. Luckily we've got his address.'

'Got a flat somewhere in Piccadilly, ain't 'e?' asked the other glumly. 'It's a tall order, guv'nor, going after him there.'

The masked man made an impatient gesture. 'It's got to be done,' he said tersely. 'He's got to be got rid of. We have the key, and if you use a silenced pistol nobody will hear. Take the car. Shelton and Harker can cover your getaway if necessary.'

'All right.' The gangster's tone was rather dubious. 'When shall we go?'

'Now!' snapped the tall man. 'You'll be in time to catch him as he comes back.'

He searched in the pockets of his long coat and pulled out the keys he had taken from Gregory at Whitegates and also one of the visiting cards. 'Here's the key and the address. Report to me here at midnight.' He nodded a curt dismissal.

'All right, guv'nor, I'll do my best.' The speaker hesitated and then went on: 'Could yer give me a shot of snow? I'm getting dithery.' He held out a shaking hand.

The masked man went over to a cupboard attached to the brick wall and unlocked it. When he came back to the table, he held in his hand a small white packet. 'Here you are,' he said contemptuously, and threw it down.

The gangster seized it as a starving animal might snatch the meat that is flung to it. 'That's better,' he said when he had sniffed the crystalline contents up his nostrils. 'Come on, you fellers. We'll go and get on with the job.'

They left the little cell-like room, and for some time after they had gone the masked man paced up and down, his chin sunk thoughtfully on his chest. Presently he went to the door and called softly. The man who had opened the trap for the other three came in answer to the summons.

'I'm going now, Gavin,' said the gang leader. 'You will get in touch with Schwartz and see that a further consignment of snow is spread round the Deptford district.'

'Yes, guv'nor.'

'And have a talk to Cornish. Find out why he didn't come last night. He'll be useful if we can only overcome his scruples. He's rather squeamish at the moment. Get him on the coke — that ought to do the trick.'

'Right you are.' The man gave an unpleasant leer. 'You'll be back here tonight?'

'Yes. We'll have to use this place for a bit, though the house at Oxshott was less risky. That's all. I'll be here about twelve.'

Gavin shuffled away to the larger cellar, and the other shut and bolted the communicating door. Going over to the other side of the small room, he unlocked a heavy iron door, stepped out onto a crazy

71

wharf, and closed the door behind him. It shut with a snap that denoted a spring lock. Raising his hands, he removed the black silk that covered his face and stuffed it into his pocket.

From the edge of the rickety landing-stage, a rough ladder led down to a small but powerful motorboat that was moored beneath. Climbing down this, the tall gang leader took his place in the boat and, starting the engine, sent it chugging up the river. There was a splash of pink in the east as he brought the trim little launch to rest at a landing-stage near Westminster and came up onto the Embankment. Hailing a taxi, he was driven to a block of flats at the upper end of Piccadilly — curiously enough, within a few hundred yards of the building in which Gregory lived.

He let himself in, ascended to the third floor in the automatic lift, and opened the door of number seven. As he did so, his tired eyes caught sight of something white stuck beneath the bronze knocker. Reaching up, he took the piece of card in his fingers, and as he saw what was written on it his sallow face went grey. There were only three words, but they were enough to send the blood ebbing from his cheeks:

'*Remember Mike Ahearn.*'

That was all. But it sent Al Brandt's mind back two years and put the fear of death in his heart!

7

The Woman in the Red Hat

Detective Inspector Shadgold was ruffled. In fact, to be perfectly candid, he was in an exceedingly bad temper. He sat beside Trevor Lowe in the police car and glowered as they drove back to town in the chill of the waking day. The shooting of Merlin under his eyes was the last straw in the series of failures he had experienced since he had pitted himself against the gang after the killing of Rosenthorne.

It had been a matter of pride with him that he had up to now refrained from seeking Trevor Lowe's help. Again and again the dramatist, with his keen insight, had helped him when he was struggling with a difficult case, and this time he had wanted to do the job off his own bat. This was the result.

In his mind's eye he saw himself

making his report to the chief commissioner, and the picture was decidedly
unpleasant. That official would have a lot
to say about the matter, and not one word
be complimentary. Shadgold had suffered
from the lash of Sir Douglas Tring's
tongue before.

Both he and Lowe had made an
inspection of the wrecked car in the field
without finding anything helpful. Certainly they had the number, but it was
pretty sure to be a fake. Taking all things
into consideration, it was not surprising
that the burly inspector was unusually
glum and never opened his lips until the
driver brought the car to a standstill
outside the block of flats in which
Gregory Carr lived.

'Are you on the telephone here?' asked
Lowe as the young man got out.

Gregory nodded. 'Yes — at the
moment,' he answered, and smiled. 'I've
had the final notice, though — a week ago
— and they may cut it off any minute.'

'Things are like that, eh?' The dramatist
raised his eyebrows.

'Very much like that,' said Gregory

ruefully. 'Well, goodbye, and thanks for the lift.'

'Take care of yourself,' said Lowe. 'And if anything should happen, get in touch with the Yard at once.'

Gregory paused halfway across the pavement. 'What do you think is likely to happen?' he asked.

Trevor Lowe pursed his lips. 'Anything,' he said noncommittally. 'I'm only suggesting that you be careful. Don't forget that you're a dangerous factor to these people. You've seen them and you could recognise them again. So keep indoors as much as possible.' He nodded a farewell before Gregory could reply to this piece of advice, and the driver sent the car gliding off down Piccadilly.

Gregory entered the flats thoughtfully and had almost reached his landing before he remembered that he had no key. With a grunt of annoyance, he sent the lift down again and went in search of the porter. He found him in the basement cooking bacon for his breakfast. The man supplied him with a spare key and he once more ascended to the fifth floor.

At that moment there were just two things he wanted — a hot bath and sleep, lots of sleep. With the imminent prospect of both these needs being satisfied, he inserted the key in the lock and entered the small hall. He had barely taken two steps across the threshold when a slight sound made him swing round.

He caught sight of a fleeting glint of light on something held by a dark figure that crouched in a corner, and instinct warning him of his danger, he dropped to his knees.

There was a dull *plop-plop*, like two corks being drawn in rapid succession, accompanied by two spears of flame that stabbed the gloom, and he heard the smack of the bullets as they hit the wall behind him.

His sudden movement had undoubtedly saved his life. The shooter muttered an imprecation when he saw that his shots had missed, and Gregory saw the nickelled blob clamped to the barrel of the pistol move downwards. The man's finger was actually squeezing round the trigger when Gregory gripped the mat that covered the polished floor and gave it a sharp tug. The killer's feet slipped from under him and he fell with a crash, the pistol flying from his hand as he did so. But he was up again in a second and launched himself at Gregory, ripping out a string of oaths and expletives as he sent a sledgehammer left and right at the other's body. But neither of those blows reached their mark. Gregory had recovered his feet and sidestepped a fraction of a second before, and as the impetus of his rush sent the other blundering past him, he planted a stinging right that connected with his assailant's jaw and made him yelp with pain.

He followed it up with a battery of body punches that pounded like pistons into the other's ribs. Gregory was seeing red. In the brief glimpse he had caught of the man's face, he had recognised one of the gangsters who had been in the dining room of Whitegates, and the sight had flamed him into a furious temper. He tore into the man as though that five-foot-eight of flesh and bone was the living embodiment of every mortal thing he hated in the world. Before the fury of that rage-maddened attack, the gangster was forced to give way. He tried to put up a guard against Gregory's lightning blows, but wherever his guard was, Gregory's bunched fist was somewhere else. They cannoned into the door of the sitting-room, sending it flying open, and reeling across the intervening strip of floor beyond brought up with a crash against the centre table. It overturned, and they went with it, Gregory on top.

'Now, you ugly-faced brute,' panted Gregory, kneeling over his vanquished enemy, 'have you had enough?'

The gangster glared up at him out of his only useful eye. 'Yes, damn you,' he growled. 'Lemme alone.'

Gregory relaxed his grip and sat back on his heels, and at the same moment the other shot up his knee and caught him a smashing blow in the small of his back. Taken by surprise, Gregory went flying over his head and fell sprawling on his face. With an evil grin, the crook scrambled to his feet, pulling an ugly-looking blackjack from his pocket as he did so. 'I'll do for you yet, you swine,' he muttered savagely. As Gregory struggled to his knees, he flung an arm round his throat, and, holding him in a strangle-hold, raised the loaded rubber cosh above his head. His arm had started on its downward journey when a clear, sharp, incisive voice behind him brought it to a sudden stop in mid-air.

'Drop that or I'll shoot!'

The gangster swung round and found himself gazing into the muzzle of his own pistol held in the steady hand of a slim woman who was standing in the open doorway. Gregory saw the wide eyes, the small head surmounted by the trim red hat, and gasped. It was the mysterious lady of the preceding night!

8

The Man in the Mask

'Good morning,' he said breathlessly, regaining his feet and wiping his streaming forehead. 'I don't know how you got here or why, but I'm very glad to see you.'

'You certainly want somebody to look after you,' she said with a slight smile.

'I'm afraid I've suddenly become very unpopular with the criminal classes,' replied Gregory. 'However, we will talk presently. At the moment, if you will keep Mr. — er — Capone entertained while I nip into the kitchen and get some rope, we can make things much more comfortable.'

'Look 'ere — ' began the gangster.

'I should hate to,' Gregory interrupted. 'You've no idea what an unpleasant sight you are or you wouldn't ask.'

'What yer going ter do?' demanded the man uneasily.

'For the moment I'm going to fix you up nice and comfy with a few lengths of rope,' said Gregory. 'Not in the way you ought to be fixed up with rope, but that will come later, I hope.'

He hurried along to the kitchen, cut down a length of rope over the sink and returned to the sitting room. 'Now,' he said pleasantly, and a few seconds later the gangster was lying helpless on the floor. 'That's that,' remarked Gregory, taking the automatic from the woman's hand and surveying his prisoner with satisfaction. 'The next question is, what are we going to do with him?'

'You're wrong there,' said the woman in the red hat. 'The next question is, what are you going to do with his friends when they come to look for him?'

Gregory started. 'His friends?' he echoed.

'Look out of the window,' she retorted briefly. 'Only, be careful they don't see you.'

He crossed obediently and, cautiously pulling the curtain aside, peered out. Drawn up at the kerb opposite the entrance was an open car. At the wheel sat a muffled figure, while another man was standing on the pavement, tapping his foot impatiently. Even at that distance Gregory could recognise Joe, the man who had guarded the hall at Whitegates. He drew in his head with a jerk. 'You're right,' he announced.

'I saw them as I came up,' she said. 'I was afraid I should be too late.'

'Why did you come?' he asked curiously.

'I came to warn you of your danger,' she answered, and then added sharply: 'What are you going to do?'

Gregory had crossed to the telephone and his hand was on the receiver. 'I'm going to call Scotland Yard,' he said, 'and have these beauties arrested.'

'No, no, don't do that!' She stopped him urgently. 'Don't bring the police into it.'

He looked at her in surprise. 'Why not?' he demanded. 'They're the right people to handle the situation.'

'I'd rather you didn't,' she said, and her eyes were troubled. 'I can't explain, but I'd rather you didn't.'

She looked at him pleadingly, and Gregory reluctantly removed his hand from the telephone. 'Why should you be afraid of the police?' he asked.

'I've told you that I can't explain,' she answered.

'Well, something's got to be done.' He glanced at the bound figure of the gangster. 'I can't leave this fellow littering up the place indefinitely, to say nothing of the other two waiting outside.'

The woman bit her lip. 'Can't you keep him here until after tonight?' she suggested. 'Then you can inform the police. It won't matter then.'

Gregory's astonishment increased. 'What difference will that make?' he said. 'What's going to happen tonight?'

'I can't tell you that either.' She shook her head. 'But please do as I ask.'

He hesitated and then shrugged his shoulders. 'All right,' he said. 'I don't know what it's all about, but all right. Now what about those two down below?' He began to pace up and down, his forehead wrinkled in a frown. Suddenly he paused and grinned. 'Since we're going to use the flat as a private police station,' he remarked, 'we may as well do the job properly.' He crossed over to the man on the floor. 'Listen,' he said rapidly. 'I want those two pals of yours who are waiting outside up here, so you'll go to the window and call them.'

'Are you mad?' broke in the woman. 'What — '

'Certainly not,' interrupted Gregory. 'The idea is a brilliant one. Mr. Capone here will call his friends up, but he'll only say what I tell him to say, because I shall be behind him with this pistol. As soon as they enter the vestibule downstairs, you will keep this choice specimen quiet with the said pistol while I take a strategic position behind the front door, which I shall leave open, armed with that very appropriate cosh. One — two — ' He made an appropriate gesture. ' — and we shall have two more unique specimens to add to our collection.'

The gangster uttered a lurid oath. 'If you think I'm going to call 'em up,' he snarled, 'you've got another think comin'. I'll see you in hell first.'

'You'll certainly go there if you don't,' retorted Gregory. 'But I shall not be there to keep you company.' He untied the man's ankles and jerked him to his feet. 'Now,' he went on grimly, 'you'll do as you're told or I shall proceed to turn you into an excellent substitute for a sieve.' He emphasised each word by digging the muzzle of the automatic into the gangster's back.

The man evidently thought discretion was the better part of valour. 'All right, blast you,' he growled. 'I'll do what yer want.'

'That's the spirit,' said Gregory encouragingly. 'Nothing can be done successfully without teamwork. Now,' he said as he pushed the gangster over to the window, 'just call down and ask both your friends to come up for a moment. And don't try any funny business, or you'll be dead before you've seen the joke!'

The gangster put his head out of the window and whistled. Keeping well out of sight, Gregory prompted him, the pistol prodding gently into his ribs. At the first whistle the man on the pavement looked up.

'Come up a minute, will yer?' called the gangster. 'Both of yer,' he added at a whispered word from Gregory, 'and be quick.'

Without giving them time to argue, Gregory pulled him back into the room and transferred the automatic to the woman. 'That's all right — you've said your little piece. Now keep quiet,' he ordered.

Taking the blackjack from his pocket, he slipped out into the hall and opened the front door. Leaving it a few inches ajar, he took up his position behind it and waited. A minute passed, two, and then he heard the sound of feet on the landing and stiffened. They came nearer and he caught a whispered word.

'Wonder what the fool wants? Look, he's left the door open.'

There was a grunt in reply, and a shadow darkened the patch of light between the door and the jamb. Gregory gripped the deadly cosh more tightly. A figure stepped across the threshold, pushing the door wide, and then — *clop*! The blackjack came down with all the force of Gregory's arm on the man's head, and he collapsed without a cry. His companion close behind him gave a startled exclamation, but the cosh rose and fell again, and with a gasping grunt he went sprawling across the other.

Gregory stuffed the weighted tube back in his pocket and dragged his unconscious victims into the sitting-room. 'There,' he panted, surveying the result of his labours with satisfaction. 'That's the end of that.'

'Not quite, Mr. Carr,' said a harsh voice. 'The end will, I think, be quite different from your anticipation!'

Gregory saw the woman's face go dead white and, spinning round, found himself staring at the man who had sentenced him to death at the empty house by the crossroads!

9

The Death Trap

'Drop that gun!' snapped the man in the doorway as the woman made a movement with the pistol she still held, and the weapon slipped from her fingers at the menacing gesture of the heavy automatic with which he was covering them.

Al Brandt chuckled behind the black silk that covered his face. 'That's better,' he remarked. 'I'm afraid, Mr. Carr, that my arrival here has rather upset your plans. It's a pity — you were getting on so well.' He glanced at the two unconscious gangsters and the bound hands of the other. 'However, if it's any consolation to you, I can assure you that my presence is quite accidental. I happened to be walking inside the Green Park on the opposite side of the street when I saw Len appear at the window. Unfortunately for you, from that point of view I could also see you as well behind him! If I had been nearer the gate, I should probably have been in time to prevent the — er, casualties.'

Gregory cursed silently. If only he had had sense enough to shut the front door after disposing of the two gangsters, he couldn't have been taken by surprise. 'Well, now that you're here, what are you going to do?' he asked curtly, while his brain raced to find a way of getting out of this fresh tangle.

'I don't think there is any need for me to answer that question, is there?' replied the gang leader, shrugging his shoulders. 'There is an old saying that if you want a thing done, do it yourself.'

'I see,' said Gregory grimly. 'Your damned thugs having failed, you're going to do a little killing on your own account.'

'That crudely puts the whole matter in a nutshell,' said Al Brandt.

'Then make a start!' snarled Gregory, and, grabbing the woman's arm, he dropped suddenly behind the settee that stood between himself and the man at the door.

Plop! In spite of the lightning speed

with which he acted, Gregory felt the bullet stir his hair as it snicked within an eighth of an inch of his head. *Plop! Plop!* Two more bullets from the silenced pistol thudded into the cushioned back of the settee, but by now Gregory had grabbed the automatic that the woman had dropped and sent three answering shots in the direction of the door. He heard a yelp of pain and his lips twisted into a grin. One of the bullets had hit!

At that moment the woman gave a warning cry, and at the same moment Gregory felt a shattering blow on his elbow that numbed his arm and sent the pistol flying from his tingling fingers. Len, although he had his hands still tied, had lashed out with his heavy boot. The pain was excruciating and Gregory's right arm was useless, but he made a frantic effort to regain possession of the pistol. Len shot his foot out to trip him up, but the woman caught his ankle, and he overbalanced and fell with a crash to the floor.

'That's the stuff to give 'em,' gasped Gregory. His fingers were closing round the gun when it was snatched from his grasp, a stunning blow caught him on the side of his head, and he pitched forward on his face.

He came to himself some minutes later with an aching head and an unaccustomed stiffness about his mouth. He realised that the pain in his head was the result of the blow that had laid him out, but it was some seconds before his scattered wits informed him that the stiffness of his jaws was caused by the very efficient gag that had been thrust into his mouth and tied securely in place. Regaining the full use of his senses, he looked about him. He couldn't move hand or foot, and discovered that he had been bound to one of the armchairs. Almost facing him was the woman in the red hat in a similar position. Len and one of the gangsters whom Gregory had coshed had gone, and the masked man was talking in low tones to the other. Snatches of the conversation came to Gregory's ears: ' . . . stay too long . . . the car . . . attract attention . . . finish and clear out . . . '

It was the gang leader who was

speaking. He glanced round to find Gregory's eyes fixed on him, and came over to the chair. 'Recovered, have you?' he said with a sneer. 'Well, the next time you lose your senses, it will be for good. You've given me a lot of trouble, and you're going to pay for it — and for this.' He held up a bandaged hand. 'It would have been better for you if Len had succeeded in putting a bullet through you,' he went on, 'for the way you're going out won't be so pleasant.'

He looked at a small square black object that stood on a table near Gregory's chair and from which ran a double line of flex to somewhere behind him. Gregory eyed the thing in wonder. 'I see that you're puzzled,' chuckled Al Brandt. 'That box contains an explosive detonated by an electric spark. The beauty of it is that I shall be able to operate it from a considerable distance. It was put in the car for a very different purpose, but I have adapted it to meet the situation. These wires — ' He touched the twisted flex. ' — which I have taken the liberty of removing from your reading lamp, go to the electric plug in your wall, passing on their way through the switch that operates this ingenious arrangement. It is very simple. The end of one wire goes to the bell on your telephone, while the other — which is not connected yet — goes to the clapper. You see the idea? From miles away, if need be, I put through a call to this flat, the bell rings, the circuit is completed, and *poof!* You and your fair companion pass into eternity.'

Gregory went cold as the full meaning of the diabolical plan burst upon him, and he glanced over at the woman. She was staring with fascinated, terror-laden eyes at the square black box on the table, and in spite of the fact that their acquaintance had been brief, he felt that he could have faced death more resignedly if she were free. She caught his glance and must have sensed something of his thoughts, for the answering look she gave him set his pulse racing. He smiled encouragingly, although he knew she couldn't see it beneath the gag.

The gang leader had gone over to the mantelpiece, and now he returned with the clock, which he put down on the table so that Gregory could see the dial. 'It will no doubt add to your enjoyment to watch the time pass,' he remarked. 'I am going to connect the wire now, and then I shall leave you. In exactly twenty minutes from my going I shall call this number.'

The cool, sneering voice sent a flood of rage through Gregory, and he strained frantically at his bonds. Al Brandt saw the blood mount to his face and the veins swell at his temples, and laughed. 'It's useless struggling,' he said. 'You'd better make the best of it.'

He walked behind the chair and, picking up the loose wire, twisted the end carefully round the bell hammer of the telephone. Then he jerked his head towards the other man, who had been a silent spectator. 'Come on,' he said. 'We'll be going.' The gangster joined him at the door with alacrity, evidently only too anxious to get away from the deadly thing on the table. 'Goodbye, Mr. Carr,' said Al Brandt mockingly, pausing on the threshold. 'And remember you have only twenty minutes to live — make the most of them.' He went out and Gregory heard the front door open and shut.

From outside in Piccadilly floated the dull roar of traffic. The world was going on as usual, oblivious of the tragedy in its midst.

Tick-tock, tick-tock! With measured beat, the clock checked off the passing seconds, and with perspiration dewing his forehead Gregory watched the slow-moving hands.

Tick-tock, tick-tock! Ten minutes more, and then the shrill whirr of the telephone would herald the end. But would it? No! That last call would be drowned in the explosion that was to blow them into oblivion. They would never hear it.

10

The Phone Call

Trevor Lowe got back to his flat in Portland Place just as his housekeeper with pails and brooms was preparing to start the cleaning operations for the day. She was so used to his comings and goings at all hours that she greeted his appearance without surprise.

He was feeling a trifle tired after his wakeful night, but not tired enough to go to bed, and so making his way to the bathroom he took a bath, dressed again and went down to his study. He had plenty to do, and was writing at his desk when White came in.

'Good morning,' remarked his secretary. 'You're up early this morning.'

'So far as I am concerned, this morning is merely a continuation of last night,' replied the dramatist. 'I haven't been to bed yet.'

White raised his eyebrows. 'I thought you must have been very late,' he said. 'I never heard you come in.'

'I've only been in about two hours,' said Lowe. He laid down his pen, blotted what he had written, and swinging round in his chair gave White an account of what had happened.

The secretary whistled. 'By Jove,' he commented, 'I wish I'd been there. It sounds like a chunk of Chicago.'

'It looked very much like it, too,' replied the dramatist dryly. 'Poor Shadgold is very fed up with the whole affair. He's fallen down rather badly over this gang business.'

'Are you thinking of helping him?' asked White. He tried to make the question sound casual, but there was a note of eagerness in his voice that made Lowe smile.

'No, I'm not,' he answered, shaking his head. 'I've got quite as much work to do as I can cope with at present, without looking for more outside my legitimate business. This is a matter for the police and they must get on with it.'

Arnold White failed to conceal his disappointment. There was nothing he liked better than when Lowe put aside his legitimate work of writing and went off on his hobby. Since his association with Detective-Inspector Shadgold, that excellent man had formed a habit of bringing the more intricate cases that came his way for the dramatist's opinion; and when he succeeded in persuading Lowe to take an active part in their solution, White was delighted. However, in this particular instance he realised that Lowe was perfectly right. They were very busy just then.

'I want you to get that rough draft of the second act of the new comedy,' said the dramatist. 'We'll see if we can't get that out of the way by tonight.'

White brought it and presently was busy taking down dialogue from Trevor Lowe's dictation. They had both forgotten all about Lowe's adventures of the night when the housekeeper appeared to say that Detective-Inspector Shadgold had called.

Lowe looked at White with a slight twinkle in his eye. 'You can shut up your book,' he said. 'I rather expected a visit from Shadgold.'

'Why?' asked White.

'Because he's in a hole, and whenever he gets into a hole he comes round here,' explained the dramatist. 'Ask him to come in.' He nodded to the housekeeper, and when she had withdrawn he commented, 'I rather gather that he's been having an interview with the chief commissioner.'

Shadgold *had* been having an interview with the chief commissioner, as they learned from his own lips very soon after he had bounced into the room and flung his hard bowler hat on the settee.

'I'm sick of the whole thing,' he roared, stamping up and down, his florid face purple and his hair bristling like a porcupine. 'They make damned stupid rules about what the police are not allowed to do, and then raise the roof because they don't get results.'

Trevor Lowe smiled sympathetically. 'What's the trouble?' he asked.

'Trouble!' shouted the Scotland Yard man. 'Trouble! Everything's the trouble.' He tugged so violently at his moustache that he brought tears to his eyes. 'I've just been before the chief,' he said, stopping his pacing abruptly, 'and got hauled over the coals for last night's business. I won't tell you all he said — some of it doesn't bear repeating — but boiled down it amounts to this: I've got another week to make good, and if I can't round up this infernal gang by then the case will be taken out of my hands and given to somebody else.'

'Who probably won't get any further than you have,' remarked Lowe.

Shadgold nodded. 'That's very likely,' he said. 'I've done all I can, Mr. Lowe. I haven't left a stone unturned.' He flung himself into a chair and rubbed his close-cropped head furiously.

'I'm sure you haven't.' Trevor Lowe rose to his feet and, crossing to the mantelpiece, began to fill his pipe. 'The whole trouble, Shadgold, is that this gang business is without precedent in this country, and therefore it can't be dealt with in the usual way. It's no good going after smaller fry. It's the fountainhead — the man in control — that you want to find. Get him and stop this wholesale distribution of cocaine, and there'll be no more trouble.'

'I quite agree,' replied the Scotland Yard man gloomily. 'But how are we going to find him? I don't know who he is from Adam, except that I'm pretty sure he's an American. I've been working on those lines. I've cabled the Central Detective Office in New York and Chicago for information regarding any known gangsters who have left the country, but nothing helpful has come of it.'

There was a pause, and Shadgold fingered his moustache nervously. 'Look here, Mr. Lowe,' he went on, 'I may as well say at once what I've come round for without beating about the bush. Will you help me?'

'Round up this gang?' asked the dramatist between puffs of smoke as he lighted his pipe.

The inspector nodded. 'Yes,' he said. 'It will get me out of the chief's bad books if I can bring this business to a successful conclusion.'

Trevor Lowe frowned. He was very busy. He had on hand a play and two films that required finishing and were wanted urgently, and his inclination was to refuse. But he had a great liking for the Scotland Yard official, and Shadgold looked so dejected that it made a refusal difficult.

'It's rather out of my line,' he said at length, 'but I'll do what I can.'

The inspector positively beamed. 'That's very good of you, Mr. Lowe,' he said gratefully, 'and I shan't forget it.'

The dramatist waved away his thanks. 'The first thing we'd better do,' he said, 'is to get hold of young Carr. He may be able to give a sufficient description of the men who were at that house at Oxshott — or at least, some of them — for us to identify them. If you could pull them in, a little judicious questioning might supply us with something.'

Shadgold looked dubious. 'I doubt it,' he said. 'You heard what Merlin said? He didn't know who his boss was.'

'I'm not suggesting that they will either,' said Trevor Lowe. 'What I'm getting at is that they might be able to supply us with a jumping-off place — possibly the medium by which they receive their supply of cocaine. In any case, it's worth trying.' He turned to White. 'Look up Gregory Carr in the telephone directory — Berkeley Mansions, Piccadilly.'

White went over to the desk and rapidly turned the pages of the volume. 'Here you are,' he announced at length. 'Mayfair 17066.'

'Get through, will you, and ask him if he will come round here at once,' said Lowe, and the secretary lifted the receiver.

There was a slight delay, and then White looked round. 'The exchange says the line is temporarily out of order,' he reported with a grin.

'He hasn't paid his bill so they've cut him off,' murmured Lowe. 'Well, if the mountain won't come to Muḥammad, Muḥammad must go to the mountain.' He slipped off his dressing gown and struggled into his jacket. 'Come along, Shadgold. We'll go and see what we can learn from Carr,' he said, going to the door.

To White's disgust, he was not included in invitation, and was left behind to deal with the morning's correspondence and his notes regarding the comedy — a task at which he set to work diligently but without interest.

Trevor Lowe and Shadgold meanwhile

picked up a taxi in Portland Place and were driven to Piccadilly, where it deposited them outside the block of flats where Gregory lived. Entering the vestibule, Lowe consulted a strip of polished mahogany on which the names of the various tenants were painted in gold lettering.

'Fifth floor,' grunted Shadgold. 'Thank God there's a lift!'

They squeezed themselves into the little cage and sent it whirling upwards. Outside the door of the flat they paused and, raising his hand, the Scotland Yard man beat a loud tattoo on the knocker.

There was silence from within, and Shadgold was in the act of repeating his summons when an exclamation from Lowe stayed his hand. 'There's something wrong here, Shadgold,' said the dramatist in a low voice. 'Look at that!'

The inspector followed the direction of his eyes. On the polished brass door handle was a red smear! Trevor Lowe touched it, and when he removed his finger it was wet and sticky. 'That's blood,' he said quietly and, hearing a sound behind him, swung round. The porter was coming down the stairs. 'Have you got a key for this flat?' called Lowe sharply, and the man stopped and looked at him in surprise.

'No, I ain't,' he growled. 'Mr. Carr lost 'is key and borrowed mine this morning, and even if I 'ad I don't see what it's got ter do with you — '

Shadgold cut into the man's remarks and thrust a card under his nose. '*That's* what it's got to do with us,' he snapped. 'I believe there's something wrong in there and I'm going in to see.'

The porter's face paled and he looked scared. 'I'm sorry,' he muttered. "Ow was I ter know yer was the perlice?'

But neither Lowe nor the inspector was listening. The dramatist's shoulders were already against the door and he was exerting all his strength to force it open. Shadgold added his not inconsiderable weight, and with a sharp, rasping crack, the lock tore from its fastenings. The door flew back with a crash, precipitating Lowe and the Scotland Yard man into the little hall.

Almost facing them was a partly open

door, and, hearing a faint sound beyond, Lowe pushed it wide and stared in. In one hurried glance he took in the two bound figures in the chairs and the sinister black object with the trailing wires that stood on the table between them, and then he turned quickly to the curious porter who had followed them.

'Go and stand by the front door and see that nobody comes in,' he ordered, as an excuse to get rid of the man, and the porter reluctantly obeyed.

Lowe took a clasp-knife from his pocket, and with two slashes severed the ropes that bound Gregory and the woman; and then, turning his attention to the black thing on the table, he snapped the wires connecting it with the telephone-bell.

'Phew!' gasped Gregory, tearing the gag from his mouth and getting unsteadily to his feet. 'That's the worst half hour I've ever spent!'

Trevor Lowe nodded grimly. He was thinking of the call White had tried to put through, and what the result would have been if his secretary had been successful. 'You owe your life to the fact that you haven't paid your telephone bill,' he remarked.

'So that was it?' Gregory wiped his damp face. 'I wondered when the twenty minutes that brute gave us was up and nothing happened. They must have cut the phone off this morning.' He looked at the woman's pale face. She was rubbing her chafed wrists, and answered his glance with an apology for a smile. 'Feeling all right?' he asked.

She nodded. 'Except that — that I feel rather sick,' she said.

'How did you get like this?' demanded Shadgold. 'What happened?'

Gregory told him.

'They don't waste time,' grunted the inspector, 'and they've certainly got nerve. Would you know 'em again?'

'I'd know the three men,' said Gregory, 'but not the other fellow. He had a handkerchief tied round his face. He's got a bullet-wound in his hand, though,' he added. 'Couldn't you trace him by that?'

'So that's where the blood on your door-knob came from,' murmured Shadgold. 'Might get him that way if he went to a doctor, but I should think he'd be too clever for that — '

The woman's voice broke in. 'Do you mind if I get a glass of water?'

'I'll get you one,' said Gregory hastily, and moved towards the door, but she stopped him.

'Don't worry, I can get it myself. Your kitchen is at the end of the passage, isn't it?'

He nodded, and she went out.

'Who's your friend?' asked Shadgold, and Gregory reddened. He had been dreading that question, for he no more knew who the woman was than the man in the moon. 'Oh, that — that's — ' he stammered painfully, and then a bright thought struck him: 'That's my fiancée,' he ended quickly.

'If we can pull in those three beauties from your description, she'll be able to identify 'em, too,' said the Scotland Yard man. 'I'd like to have a word with her when she comes back.'

But she didn't come back. They waited a few minutes and then sent Gregory to fetch her, but he came back to say that she was nowhere in the flat.

Trevor Lowe went out to interview the porter. 'Yes, I saw the lady,' said the man in answer to the dramatist's question. 'She went down in the lift. In a mighty 'urry she was, too.'

'Your — er — fiancée must have had an urgent appointment,' remarked Lowe. 'Do you know where we can find her?'

Gregory stared at him without answering. He hadn't the least idea where the woman in the red hat was to be found, and he was racking his brains to think of some sensible answer to give to the dramatist's question.

11

What Mr. Marlow Knew

Gregory's rather uncomfortable predicament was ended, however, for the moment by an exclamation from the sitting room and the appearance of Shadgold at the door. 'Here, Mr. Lowe!' cried the inspector. 'I've found something. Come and look at this!'

Trevor Lowe joined him, and Shadgold held out a torn scrap of paper. 'I found this on the floor by the settee,' he explained. 'It may be a clue — unless,' he added, suddenly turning to Gregory, 'it's yours.'

Gregory looked at the dirty slip and shook his head. 'No, it's not mine,' he answered. 'It must have come out of one of those fellows' pockets.'

'That's what I thought,' said Shadgold. 'It looks like part of a message. See these pencilled words?'

Lowe had already taken the piece of

paper from his hand and was reading the sprawling writing: 'Tonight . . . stuff . . . ged Ship . . . bar.'

'What do you make of it?' asked the Scotland Yard man. 'Looks as though it was an appointment to meet on some ship or other.'

The dramatist frowned, and then his brow suddenly cleared. 'No, I don't think this refers to a ship,' he answered. 'I think I know what it means.'

'What?' asked Shadgold eagerly.

'Have you ever heard of The Full-rigged Ship?' said Lowe, and when the inspector shook his head: 'It's a public house near the docks in Deptford, mostly frequented by sailors and seafaring men. It's got a none-too-savoury reputation, and I wouldn't mind betting that it's the place this scrap of paper refers to.'

'Near the docks, is it?' said Shadgold. 'I wonder if the 'stuff' means dope?'

'Quite probably, I should say,' replied Lowe. 'It's a very likely place to find cocaine runners. This fellow who's distributing the stuff wholesale must be getting his supplies from somewhere. If we could discover how, it might give us a line to the man himself.'

'You're right,' said Shadgold, nodding in agreement. 'There's evidently something happening there tonight. I'll get hold of some good men and put them onto the place, and — '

'I wouldn't do that,' broke in the dramatist. 'The finding of this clue is a chance in a thousand, and you don't want to spoil it.'

'Spoil it! What do you mean?' demanded the inspector in surprise.

'Well,' Lowe said, smiling, 'with all due respect for your fellows at the Yard, Shadgold, you can spot 'em as detectives a mile off. If they're seen hanging about in the neighbourhood of the Full-rigged Ship, these birds will get alarmed and steer clear of the place, and we shall be no better off. You'd better leave this to me.'

Shadgold pursed his lips undecidedly. 'There's a lot of truth in what you say. But if you are thinking of going there on your own, it's a big risk, Mr. Lowe.'

The dramatist's smile broadened. 'One's life is full of risks,' he answered, 'and so long as I'm not recognised there isn't even a risk — and I don't think I shall be recognised.'

'Well, it's damned good of you,' grunted Shadgold, 'but I don't like — '

'I said I'd help, and I'm going to,' replied Lowe. 'So let's leave it at that.'

The Scotland Yard man shrugged his shoulders. 'All right,' he said. 'But I shall feel happier when you get back.'

He took his departure presently, leaving Lowe and Carr alone, and after a few seconds' silence the dramatist turned to the young man. 'Now then,' he said quietly, 'let's hear all about it.'

'All about what?' asked Gregory innocently, though he knew perfectly well what Lowe was driving at.

'Who was the woman?' demanded Lowe.

'My fiancée — ' began Gregory, but the dramatist interrupted him.

'It's no good trying to pull that stuff on me,' he said. 'Come on, who was she?'

Gregory thought desperately to try and find a plausible story, and, failing, resorted to the truth.

'I guessed you were hiding something,' commented Lowe when he'd finished. 'Nature didn't provide you with the right kind of face for lying.'

Gregory smiled. 'I'm sure the woman has got nothing to do with this gang,' he said. 'I don't know why she wouldn't let me get on to the police, but I'm certain it's not for a criminal reason.'

'Perhaps she doesn't like the cut of the uniform,' said Lowe sarcastically. 'I know of only one reason, my friend, for people not liking the police, and that is because they've got something to hide.'

'But if she had anything to do with the gang,' protested Gregory, 'why should they have tried to put her out of the way? Besides, none of them had ever seen her before — I'm certain of that.'

'You're certain of a good many things,' retorted the dramatist, 'but I'm only certain of one — and that is that you ought to have told me all about this woman before. She's probably in possession of knowledge that would be of vital importance in getting on the track of the fellow who is running this bunch. I'm not sure that you ought not to be arrested for conspiring to defeat the ends of justice.'

He left Gregory full of misgivings, but quite unshaken in his faith in the mysterious lady with the red hat, and walked back to Portland Place. He was turning the key in the lock of the front door when some instinct made him swing round, and the knife which had been intended for his back buried itself in the woodwork to the depth of nearly two inches!

He caught a momentary glimpse of the would-be killer, and then the man took to his heels and jumped aboard a slow-moving car that was crawling along by the kerb. Before Lowe could raise an alarm, it put on speed and was lost around the first corner.

The dramatist wrenched the knife from the door and carried it thoughtfully into the house.

'Quite an unpleasant interlude,' he remarked later after he had finished explaining the incident to Arnold White. 'And now let's see what we can do with that second act. I want to work on that this afternoon because I've got rather a busy evening before me.'

★ ★ ★

Detective-Inspector Shadgold glanced at a note on his desk and, stretching out a hand, pressed a button. Of the messenger who came in answer to his ring, he enquired if Sergeant Collins was in.

'I think so, sir,' said the constable.

'Tell him I want to see him,' grunted Shadgold.

After a little delay, Sergeant Collins made his appearance. He was a tall, thin man with a remarkably large nose and remarkably small eyes. He stood in front of Shadgold's desk and waited for his superior to speak.

'I've had a message from a Mr. Leopold Marlow,' said the inspector. 'He's got something of importance to say, or says he has. He wouldn't hint what it was on the telephone. Go round and see him, will you? Here's his address.' He scribbled it down on a slip of paper and pushed it across the desk to the sergeant.

'You can apologise for my not going myself. Say that I'm very busy, but that if it's anything important I'll come along.'

Sergeant Collins picked up the slip of paper, put it into his pocket, and enquired if there was anything else.

'No, that's all,' said Shadgold. 'Get along there as quickly as you can.'

The sergeant left the office and walked down the stairs to the Whitehall entrance to Scotland Yard. Here he boarded a bus which took him to Hyde Park Corner. A policeman on point duty showed him the way to Darnley Court Mansions, which proved to be a turning just before the Knightsbridge Galleries. The building had been converted into luxury service flats, and as Sergeant Collins went up in the lift to the second floor, he wondered what it was Mr. Marlow was so anxious to talk about, and why he had refused to give any hint of his business over the telephone.

Number seven was right at the end of the corridor. In reply to the sergeant's knock, the door was opened by a short, thick-set man in a dinner jacket who was smoking a cigar. He had a bullet head, bald and shiny on the top, and heavy features whose moist, unhealthy pallor added to the surliness of the eyes and the loose, rather brutal mouth.

Sergeant Collins instinctively took a dislike to the man. 'Do you happen to be Mr. Marlow?' he enquired.

'Yes, I do. What do you want?' The man was frowning and didn't trouble to hide the fact.

'I've come from the Yard,' said Collins, and explained who he was.

Mr. Marlow rolled a cigar to the other side of his mouth and appeared to be rather annoyed. 'I wanted to see Inspector Shadgold himself, but now you're here I suppose you'd better come in,' he said with the air of one trying to make the best of a very poor substitute.

He ushered the sergeant into a large, softly lighted room with dark oak furniture and thick Turkish rugs on the polished floor. At one end of the apartment was a massive bookcase with glass doors, through which could be seen rows of new and expensively bound volumes; not one, however, looking as if it had been read.

Mr. Marlow closed the door and came over to the fireplace, where he stood with his hands clasped behind his back.

'You can tell Inspector Shadgold from me,' he remarked, 'that I don't admire the way he treats people who want to do him a good turn.'

'The inspector's very busy at the moment, sir,' said Collins.

Mr. Marlow's mouth twisted cynically at the corners. 'Well, it's his funeral,' he grunted. 'I'm leaving the country tomorrow.'

The sergeant looked a little bewildered. 'I'm sorry, sir,' he said, 'but I don't quite understand.'

Mr. Marlow turned and slowly took the cigar from his mouth. With his other hand he produced from the pocket of his jacket a folded piece of note-paper which he held out towards Collins. 'Read that,' he said.

The Yard man unfolded the note and glanced at the contents. There was neither address nor signature, and the message was typewritten. It ran:

'Out of your many business ventures, you have made over a quarter of a million pounds, though you have deluded the income tax authorities into believing your portion to be only half this amount. The penalty for making false income tax returns is a long stretch of imprisonment. The penalty for ignoring this letter is death.

'If you wish to remain alive, you will have to pay to the extent of half your entire fortune. Have this sum in bearer bonds by three a.m. Thursday when a taxi will call. The driver will have been given instructions, so do not question where you are being driven to. If you disobey or seek any sort of assistance, you will be killed.'

Sergeant Collins looked up quickly. 'When did you get this, sir?'

'Yesterday morning,' said Mr. Marlow, 'by the first post.'

'Is that true about the income tax, sir?' asked Collins, and the other gave a short hard laugh.

'True? Of course, it isn't true,' he

121

snapped, but the sergeant knew that he was lying. 'That note,' went on the man, 'came from the same bunch that got Abraham Rosenthorne. But they're not going to get me, because I'm clearing out of the country tomorrow until everything's blown over. But — ' He paused and wagged his finger impressively. 'before I go, I've got something to say that will put 'em in queer street. I know something, but I'm not spilling a word to anyone except Inspector Shadgold.' He stopped and took a deep breath. 'There, you can tell Shadgold that. I shall be here up to midday tomorrow, and if he likes to call I'll tell him something worth knowing.'

'I think it would be safer if you told me now, sir,' suggested the sergeant, but Mr. Marlow shook his head firmly.

'No, I'm not talking to anyone but Shadgold himself,' he asserted.

'I wish you'd given some hint of this when you rang him up, sir,' said Collins. 'The inspector might have found time to slip along.'

'Yes, I dare say. He tried that game

himself, but I wasn't having any. I don't like the telephone for confidences.' Mr. Marlow broke off with a smooth chuckle and helped himself to another cigar, which he took from a large silver box standing under the lampshade on a small Benares table. As he held the match and puffed at the cigar, the flame cast yellow flickering shadows across his face and gave him an expression of almost bland complacence quite out of keeping with the shadow of death that lurked ready to strike him down should he disobey those written commands.

Collins rose to his feet and reached for his hat. 'I'll tell the inspector what you say, and in any case I expect he'll give you a ring in the morning.'

A moment later he was shown out of the flat and was descending to the ground floor in the lift. As he stepped out onto the pavement, he noticed a saloon car drawn up to the kerb on the other side of the road fifty yards or so lower down. Without heeding, Collins walked briskly towards the main thoroughfare and jumped onto a bus going in the direction of Whitehall. It was nine o'clock, and he was going to have some food before returning to Scotland Yard.

As he sat on top of the bus, he fell to wondering what the inspector would do about Mr. Marlow, and what it was that gentleman had up his sleeve. Here most unexpectedly was another point of contact with the gang. Marlow obviously knew something, and the inspector would most certainly be interested in that. Collins decided to forgo his food until after he had made his report, and he smiled as he wondered how Mr. Marlow would appeal to his brusque superior.

But he need not have wondered. Although Inspector Shadgold was destined to meet Mr. Leopold Marlow, it was not as the latter had planned.

12

The Crimson Letter

Mr. Leopold Marlow tilted the decanter till his glass was two-thirds full of brandy, then added soda to the brim, and with lacklustre eyes watched the effervescence die down till only a few speck-like bubbles floated to the surface of the amber-coloured liquid and dispersed with a faint hissing sound. He turned the glass slowly in his hand and noted with inward satisfaction that the movement was steady as a rock. Yes, it certainly took more than a bunch of gangsters to upset his nerves!

The idea seemed to please him immensely, and caused a loose smile to creep across the lower part of his sallow face. Suddenly, lifting his arm and throwing back his bullet head, he drained the glass dry and put it back on the tray. Turning on his heel, he went over to the corner of the room and sat down heavily before the open bureau with his back to the door. The loose smile still played on his lips as he stared fixedly at the ink-stand. It was a massive ornamental affair made of solid black marble, with two silver-mounted wells on either side of an upright perpetual calendar, the white ivory disc of which announced Tuesday, January 19.

The day after tomorrow would be Thursday, the day mentioned in the letter. But by that time he would be well away. They'd have a bit of a shock when they found he'd been so smart — especially Anstruther, as he called himself. Well, it would serve him right, and he'd get his deserts.

Letting his thoughts continue in the same vein, Mr. Marlow leaned forward and automatically twiddled the black knob of the calendar with his finger and thumb. It was, of course, rather a nuisance having to leave the country at such short notice, but it was infinitely better than the alternative. Also, it would be rather amusing in the quiet seclusion of Paris reading in the London newspapers how Anstruther had been rounded up on the strength of information that he, Marlow, had left behind. When the coast was clear he could come home again, but he'd have to watch that tax business.

A momentary frown clouded his brow. If this Shadgold fellow wanted to be nasty, he could make things pretty unpleasant — but would he? At the back of his mind, Mr. Marlow was inclined to think that what he had to tell would counterbalance that other matter. In any case, it would be extremely difficult to prove anything; he'd covered his tracks too carefully for that.

With a muttered exclamation, he pulled himself out of his reverie and started going through a bundle of papers. Some of them he put in a drawer at his side, and some he merely glanced at, tore up and threw into the wastepaper basket.

After a while he got up and went to the adjoining bedroom, where Jelf had already packed his trunks prior to receiving a curt dismissal from the services of Mr. Marlow, to whom he had been valet for the past six months.

Presently he came back with a letter in

his hand, and sitting down at the bureau again, searched for a stamp. Affixing one, he reached over and pressed the bell-push in the wall. While he waited, he leaned sideways in his chair and glanced casually through the narrow parting of the curtains on his immediate right. Down in the street below he caught a glimpse of a dark saloon car standing by the lamp-post on the opposite side of the road — and then came a knock at the outer door.

'Come in!' called Marlow over his shoulder.

The door clicked open, and the lift attendant came silently across the thick pile carpet.

'I want you to post this letter,' Mr. Marlow told him. 'It's urgent.'

The man took the letter, and was about to withdraw when Mr. Marlow called him back. 'By the way, is the housekeeper in?' he asked, and on being told he wouldn't be back until eleven o'clock added: 'Well, I'd like to have a word with him tonight.'

'Yessir!' The attendant nodded and deferentially took his departure.

When he had gone, Mr. Marlow

continued his clearance of the desk, and presently became so engrossed in this occupation that he failed to hear the outer door open with a faint creak. Something, however, caused him to glance up, and he saw, reflected in the leaded glass doors of the bookcase forming the upper part of the bureau, a sight that sent the blood draining from his cheeks and made his eyes bulge with fear. His jaw dropped, and as he clutched the arms of the chair he made a hoarse, inarticulate sound in his throat — and then:

Plop! Plop! Plop! Plop!

The figure standing by the door fired four times with the silenced gun he held, and each bullet found its mark in the square fleshy back of the man seated at the desk. He uttered a sharp groan, and slumped forward with one hand groping at his blood-stained shirt-front where one bullet had passed right through.

The man who had killed him slipped the smoking weapon into his pocket and hurried silently from the flat. He darted from the building just as the lift attendant was returning from the post, and, bounding across the road, jumped into the waiting car and slammed the door with a bang.

With wide eyes, the liftman watched the rapidly receding car until it had vanished into the darkness. Then he went inside, much puzzled and scratching the hair behind his left ear. 'That bloke was in a hurry, an' no mistake!' he muttered.

Shortly after eleven o'clock, Mr. Jones, the housekeeper, came up the steps a little uncertainly, and smelling rather strongly of beer. He made for the lift and nodded to the attendant. 'No messages, I suppose?' he asked.

'Yes, one from Mr. Marlow,' said the liftman, jerking the gates to. 'He says he wants to 'ave a word with you tonight, and will you go and see him.'

As the lift soared upwards, Mr. Jones instinctively spruced himself up and adjusted his collar and tie. Five minutes later, after a quick wash and brush-up, he came out of his own apartments on the top floor and made his way down to No. 7. He found the door standing ajar and tapped politely. There was no answer.

'Shall I step in, sir?' he said softly, at the same time pushing the door open slightly and peering round. The shaded electric lamp on the small Benares table by the fireplace was still on, but there was only a faint glimmer in the grate, which contained a heap of white ashes. Glancing quickly about him, Mr. Jones started visibly at the sight of the slumping figure in the armchair in front of the bureau. He went forward quickly, and had taken only a few paces before he saw the bullet holes that had been neatly drilled into Mr. Marlow's back. The blood had oozed and stained the black vicuna of his dinner-jacket in crimson circlets about the four separate wounds.

Mr. Jones pulled up with a jerk, his fingers twitching nervously as he gaped open-mouthed, half hypnotised by his gruesome find. Blood had trickled onto the floor in little pools. Dazedly he noticed that the dead man's head, turned partly sideways so that the glazed eyes stared back at him, rested on the desk itself and was supported at the back by the right arm, the bloodstained fingers of

131

which sprawled over the blotting pad. The near arm hung down limply by the dead man's side.

Mr. Jones recoiled from the stark horror written in those sightless eyes and backed unsteadily towards the door. With each yard he put between himself and the horrible thing at the bureau, his courage came slowly back; and simultaneously with his exit, he found his voice and began shouting the place down.

★ ★ ★

In front of a comfortable fire in Trevor Lowe's cosy study at Portland Place, Arnold White sat in slippered ease, deep in the concluding chapters of a particularly exciting novel. The room was very quiet, with only the clock on the mantelpiece breaking into the faint crackle from the grate.

White finished his book, threw it down, and, lighting a cigarette, glanced at the clock. It was twelve fifteen, and he frowned slightly. Surely it was high time Trevor Lowe had come back. He was in the act of crossing over to the window when the telephone bell shattered the stillness and brought him quickly over to the instrument. He jerked up the receiver and heard an anxious familiar voice.

'Hello. Is that Mr. White? This is Shadgold speaking. Is Mr. Lowe there?'

The secretary explained Lowe's absence and heard the inspector growl something under his breath. 'When will he be back?'

'Haven't the foggiest,' said White. 'What's in the wind? You sound thoroughly worked up about something.'

'Can't tell you over the phone,' came back Shadgold's sharp staccato tones. 'Can I come round to wait for Mr. Lowe? . . . Right. I'll be along in about twenty minutes.'

He rang off, and Arnold White went back to the window with a pleasurable feeling of excitement. Something had happened, and apparently something pretty big, for Shadgold did not usually let things get underneath his skin to that extent.

The housekeeper had gone to bed, so White had to go downstairs himself and let the inspector in when he presently arrived in a taxi. When he had been escorted into the study, Shadgold faced White grimly.

'Something drastic will have to be done,' he said vehemently. 'These infernal gangsters put another victim on the spot tonight — in a block of flats near Hyde Park Corner — and got clean away with it. He'd had the usual note demanding money, and was thinking of bolting from the country, but they got him. Four places in the back and one bullet right through.'

'Who was the fellow?' asked White.

'A man called Leopold Marlow,' answered the inspector. 'He knew something, too. Phoned me up this morning.' He explained to the interested White the result of Collins's interview. 'The gangsters were on the watch,' he concluded, biting his moustache almost viciously, 'and saw Collins come and go. That was the death signal for Marlow.'

'How was it done?' queried White, a little shocked.

'They came in a car,' explained the Yard man, 'and one of 'em slipped in and did the shooting while the lift attendant was out posting a letter for Marlow. When the liftman came back, he almost bumped into the assassin on his way up, but of course he never suspected.' He paused and frowned thoughtfully. 'Marlow apparently didn't die instantaneously, as might have been expected, but lingered long enough to be able to scrawl on the blotting pad with his blood-stained finger the letter 'A.' I'm wondering whether he was trying to leave some sort of a clue. Something connected with what he was going to tell me.'

'I should think it was quite likely,' breathed White, 'but a single letter 'A' doesn't help much. It might mean anything.'

'Yes, that's true,' said Shadgold. 'Perhaps Mr. Lowe will be able to suggest something.'

White looked round anxiously at the clock. 'I wish to goodness he was here,' he muttered half under his breath, but loud enough for the Yard man to hear.

Quite unconsciously he had voiced the exact and very sincere thoughts of Trevor Lowe himself, who, at that precise moment, was far removed from the homely comforts of Portland Place.

13

The Message in the Box

Dusk was falling when there came into the bar of the Full-rigged Ship a lighter-man fresh from his barge. Years of toiling labour at the big sweeps had left their callouses, and the corns on his hands were ingrained with dirt. He wore a blue jersey that came high up to the neck, and about his throat was twisted a loose silk scarf. His coat was of blue serge, and his trousers were ever so slightly bellied at the bottoms. One hand was thrust into his pocket, raising the hem of his jersey a little, and beneath showed the curve of a leather belt shiny with hard wear, and marvellously adorned with brass insignia and crests. A large peaked cap that did not quite hide the wisp of plastered quiff over his forehead, and a pair of squeaky brown boots, completed the picture.

He strolled quietly up to the counter

and ordered a pint of bitter. The barman pulled his drink and went on polishing glasses, with but a casual glance.

The newcomer edged his way to a corner of the bar from whence he could survey the whole place, put his foot on the brass rail, and, propping himself up on one elbow, became lost in contemplation of the foam on his beer.

'Busy?' asked the potman conversationally, polishing away industriously.

Trevor Lowe shrugged his shoulders. 'So-so,' he replied. 'Nothing grand. Bit quiet on the river these days.'

'So they all say.' The potman nodded. 'What's your line — grain?'

'Cement.' The dramatist finished his drink and pushed the tankard across the counter to be refilled.

There was safety in cement. All the big cement companies ran their own barges, and they carried nothing but cement from one year's end to another. Cement men knew nothing else of river life except the steady transportation of the stuff from one point to another. Their job never varied. If they didn't join in the more general conversations of diversified shop, it was excusable, for they had little to offer to the common fund of small talk. Cement men handled the big seagoing barges, and were often moving around the coast for weeks at a time.

It was early yet, and the place which possessed only one bar, common to all classes, was but sparsely filled. Two women, with their husbands' caps pinned over straggly hair, were having a heated altercation concerning the clothes-line rights over a parting fence. A couple of men near Lowe were discussing a betting transaction that reflected on the honesty of one Bill.

As the evening drew on, however, the place began to fill up, and the dramatist kept a sharper lookout. He was in the dark as to what was likely to happen; was in complete ignorance of the identity or appearance of the person or persons for whom the message had been intended. He could only trust to luck that some suspicious happening would betray the people he was there to find.

The bar filled up with a noisy, chattering throng, and the air became hazy with

138

strong tobacco-smoke; but there was nothing to warrant Lowe picking on any particular one of the different species of humanity present. The dramatist ordered another drink.

'Matches — laces — studs. Buy a box of matches?'

Lowe set down his half-empty mug as the plaintive voice reached his ears, and looked round in the direction of the sound. A beggar had entered and was shuffling round, displaying his wares on a dilapidated tray. 'Matches — laces?' he quavered in a thin reedy voice, pausing before each little group expectantly.

A few dropped a coin into the tray, and the man intoned his thanks. Then a rough-looking fellow who was lounging against the bar in the opposite corner called to him. "'Ere, I'll 'ave a box of matches, mate,' he said, and the beggar went over to him.

It was only a slight thing that caused Lowe's eyes to narrow suddenly and made his pulse quicken. There were half a dozen boxes of matches on the tray, but the beggar selected none of these for his new customer. His hand dipped down behind a card of cheap studs, and he produced the box he held out from there.

'Thank you, sir,' he mumbled as the other took it, flung tuppence onto the tray, and slouched away.

Lowe's brain worked quickly. Was there anything significant in the incident? It seemed peculiar that this special box of matches should have been brought out from behind the card. He watched keenly, and saw the recipient of the matches produce a packet of cigarettes and place one between his lips. Putting the packet back in his pocket, he opened the matchbox and fumbled for a match, and as he extracted one Lowe saw something white slipped quickly from the box to the palm of his hand.

The dramatist drained his mug. His suspicions had been correct. A message of some description had been conveyed in that box. The beggar was making his way to the swing-doors, and Lowe had to decide quickly whether he would follow him or concentrate his attention on the other man. He chose the latter. The beggar had, after all, delivered his message, and was probably not worth following. So Lowe let him go without even a casual glance.

The other man smoked his cigarette through to the end, and ordered another drink.

'Time, gentlemen, please,' sang out the raucous voice of the bartender. The man gulped down the glass of rum that was pushed towards him and made for the door. Lowe leisurely followed suit. The man was in the act of crossing the road as the dramatist came out of the swing-doors; and after pausing for a second and glancing to left and right, Lowe went after him.

He turned down a side-turning and entered a maze of narrow streets, doubling and twisting till Lowe himself had lost all idea of his own direction. He knew he was somewhere near the river, for the dank river smells eddied up from blind side-turnings, and welled coldly in his face from black alleys that sloped away down into the silent darkness.

They were in a neighbourhood of gloomy-looking warehouses that towered up above them and merged into the night overhead. Here and there solitary gas-jets flickered yellowly, casting dim pools of murky light for a few yards around and making the surrounding blackness seem even blacker. There was not a sound save the soft shuffle of the man ahead as he padded along the empty streets. A wall of silence seemed to envelop the place.

Here the slums, with their thickly infested life, had given way to the commercial areas of dockland. There were other smells in the air now besides those of the river. The piney scent of pitch gave a pungency to the general mealy reek of grain that hung heavily in the air. Presently it was the rather acrid smell of bacon that came drifting out of a great darkened curing factory, and farther on a dozen different grades of cheese stung the nostrils. High-scented toilet preparations warred with the rich aromas of roast coffee, and through it all there was a muted note: the unmistakable, indefinable smell of ships' upper decks — rope, oakum, engine-oil, and the tang of dead steam.

The man ahead swung sharply away to the right and entered a long, gloomy alley.

142

It was narrow and cobbled, and so cramped that the buildings on either side almost leaned against one another. Trevor Lowe slowed down and peered ahead. His quarry had vanished in the darkness. It was a locality where night prowlers turned out the street-lamps almost as soon as they had been lit, and the dramatist was completely out of his bearings. The soft, shuffling step ahead ceased. Lowe listened, but no sound came to his ears, and then very faintly and muffled he heard the thud of a closing door.

He went cautiously down the alley, looking from side to side at the bleak walls of the buildings that hemmed it in. Not a glimmer of light showed; not a sound came from within those dirt-grimed walls. There were several windows, but lengths of sacking were hung against the sashes inside, and he couldn't see through.

He came to a door, but it looked as though it had not been used for years. The dust was crusted thickly into the crevices, and the letter-box had been boarded up. Further along was a high gate big enough to admit a lorry. Lowe paused. He had come out of the alley into a broad thoroughfare, but he was convinced that the man he had been following had not come so far. By some way or other he had gone into that huge deserted-looking building on the right. Lowe knew there must be some way into the place other than the big gates, but he judged that he had neither the time nor the opportunity in the dark of finding it. He decided to take his chances in both hands and go over the top of the gate.

It was a high gate, and there were spikes along the top of it, but in five minutes he was on the other side and creeping across a store yard. The whole place in the rear was in a ruinous state of dilapidation, and Lowe realised that it was a derelict warehouse he was in. Great doors hung on their hinges above tumbledown platforms that had once been used as loading quays for drays. The entrances had been barricaded up, but even the barricades were falling to pieces. Windows gaped open, and broken panes were stuffed with rags. It was a mournful picture of desolation. He found a rotted door and climbed inside, stopping on the threshold to listen.

Rats, unseen in the blackness, went scurrying away, squeaking shrilly. A dusty smell of rot and decay filled the place; the whole building seemed to be creaking with age. Lowe went forward further, feeling his way foot by foot. Presently he came up against a wall, and had to pull out his torch. He stuck the thin paper wrapping from some cigarettes over it to minimise the glare, and went on.

The place was a veritable warren. Cross-passages seemed to lead off at every other yard, and now and then he emerged into a vast room whose deserts of space echoed emptily back at him.

Lowe could hear no sign of the man he had been following, but his sensitive nerves reacted to a feeling of foreboding. It was as though the place was waiting for something. His imagination pictured eyes up among the dust-laden rafters, eyes that followed him from room to room and peered down silently from the yawning holes in the ceiling where the plaster had fallen.

He used the torch only sparingly,

fearful that its faint glimmer would be seen. The building seemed to have neither beginning nor end. He had just decided to try and work his way back to the place he had entered and start over again, when all in a second it happened. He was feeling his way along in the dark when suddenly he put out his foot and stepped into space!

Sheer and plumb he fell, his body still upright, his right foot still out in the act of walking. With the natural nerve reaction of a sudden crisis, his muscles flexed. He tensed in every tissue, and the next moment he landed with a body-shaking smash that knocked the breath out of him.

14

The Snow Man

For some seconds Trevor Lowe lay where he had fallen. His leg was doubled up under him, and was paining him horribly, but otherwise he felt very much the same as he had done before he stepped over the brink.

He still retained his grasp of the torch, and pressing the button he sent a ray of light travelling slowly about him. He was lying on a huge mound of cotton waste, mildewed and oil-soaked. The soft glow showed the sides of a shaft going up into the blackness above. They seemed to streak up into infinity.

Gradually he got his mind back, and found that his leg had ceased to hurt and was now numb. He moved carefully, but the limb was useless. Falling on it must have wrenched it badly.

Suddenly he switched off the light and

lay still. From somewhere close at hand came the dull rumbling of voices, and he realised why he had been stumbling about so long without finding a clue to the man he had been following. The gang's hide-out was buried deep down in the basements under the road level.

He had come a fearful cropper down the shaft, but he was thankful for the accident. Except for that, he might have gone blundering about all night up there in the emptiness without finding his quarry.

To his right was the lift entrance to the shaft, the woodwork broken and the iron struts rusty and twisted, and it was through that opening that the voices were coming. He couldn't hear what was being said, only a low murmur.

He stood up, trying his weight gingerly on his injured leg. A sharp, stabbing pain went searing through his thigh, but with an effort it stood the strain. He concluded that he had wrenched a tendon, and began to massage the limb vigorously. In a few seconds the sharp, stabbing pain gave way to a dull ache, and although he was forced to limp slightly he no longer felt afraid that the leg would not support him.

He hobbled out of the shaft and took his bearings. Ahead stretched a wide stone passage, at the end of which came a dim trickle of light from a partly opened door. The voices came from this direction, and there seemed to be a sort of conference going on, though Lowe couldn't hear a single word that was being said.

He was cautiously approaching that partly opened door when a bell tinkled softly inside the room, and the low murmur of conversation ceased abruptly.

Lowe experienced a sudden premonition of danger. A second door stood almost opposite him on his right, and, trying the handle and finding that it was open, Lowe stepped inside. He wasn't a moment too soon, for he had scarcely time to close the door behind him before he heard the sound of approaching footsteps, and, peering out through the narrow slit of the frame, he made out the figure of the man he had followed from the Full-rigged Ship coming along the passageway.

Lowe hazarded a guess as to the meaning of the bell. The meeting was not yet complete, and the man was going up to admit the missing member of the gang. There was nothing for it but to wait until he had returned. It would be too risky to attempt to get a glimpse inside that other room with the possibility of the fellow returning and taking him by surprise. In the meanwhile, he explored round the room in which he had taken refuge.

The light of his torch revealed it as a big stockroom with wooden shelves running round all four sides, with the exception of the space for the door. They were filled with large square tins, and Lowe examined them, his forehead puckered in a frown. They were tins of ships' biscuits. He fumbled among them until he found one that was broken, and taking out a biscuit, twisted it about in his fingers. There was nothing strange about it; it was just an ordinary biscuit of the kind that is supplied in thousands to ships that are ill-equipped with baking facilities.

He broke it, and his eyes gleamed as the secret of the biscuits was revealed. The outer crust of baked flour crumbled away in his hand, and he found himself holding an oblong case of tin as thin and narrow as a cigarette-case. He tried to find some way of opening it, but the joints had been soldered, and without some form of cutter it was impossible. But he knew what the tin contained. This room down in the basement of the disused warehouse was a vast cocaine store, and it was from here that the unknown gang leader drew the supplies with which he was slowly flooding the underworld.

Lowe slipped the slim tin, together with two more of the biscuits, into his pocket, and then stiffened as he heard the sound of footsteps coming back along the wide passage. Creeping softly to the door, he applied his eye to the crack. The dancing light of a torch was approaching, and in its dim rays he saw the muffled figures of two men, preceded by the man who had evidently gone up to admit them in answer to the signal of the bell.

They proceeded in silence past the

151

door behind which the dramatist was hiding, and disappeared through the other at the end of the corridor. Lowe heard a voice raised in greeting, and then the door was shut, cutting off all sound.

Lowe waited for a moment or two to make sure that the coast was clear, and then he stepped quietly out into the passage and crept towards the closed door. A single star-point of light shot out from the darkness, and he guessed that it came from the keyhole. The key therefore was either not in the lock or had been so turned as to leave the aperture free. In either case, where light could shine out, Lowe could see in, and he was very anxious to get a glimpse of the interior of that room and its occupants.

He reached the door and, bending down, applied his eye to the keyhole. He could see three quarters of the room beyond, and all four of the people in it. Behind a rough table on which stood a lighted hurricane lamp was seated one of the fattest and most repulsive-looking men that Lowe had ever seen. His huge bulk bulged over the sides of the chair on which he sat, and his shining, flabby face, moist and dead-white in colour, rested on an enormous cupped hand like a full moon. His eyes, small and beady, were sunk among folds of flesh, and his mouth, small and red-lipped, looked like a spot of blood on a bladder of lard. He was looking across the table at the other three men, who stood together in a group facing him. Presently, as Lowe watched, his mouth moved and the words, muffled but distinguishable, reached the dramatist's ears.

'I'm glad you have come, Cornish.' The sentence was as calm and as placid as a summer pool, but Lowe experienced a sudden chill in the region of his spine, for there was an undercurrent at the back of it that was quivering with wickedness. It was as though the fat man had silently added: 'Because if you hadn't, I should have been under the painful necessity of fetching you.'

The man addressed as Cornish — a slim, pale-faced, ill-looking youth — was one of the two newcomers; and as the other spoke, he passed a tongue across hot, dry lips. 'I didn't want to come, Mr. Schwartz,' he muttered. 'I'd rather not have anything to do with it. Why can't you leave me alone?'

Schwartz shrugged his shoulders. 'I am only obeying orders,' he replied. 'I am not the one who does the planning in these matters. The boss's instructions are that you are to be entrusted with the Bond Street job, and if you don't carry out his wishes you know what to expect.'

Cornish made a gesture of despair. 'I'd rather not have anything to do with it,' he said again. 'I'm not made for this sort of game. I haven't got the nerve. For God's sake, leave me out of it and get somebody else!'

Schwartz made a smooth, deprecatory movement with his hands. 'I am sorry,' he purred softly in his oily, slightly guttural voice, 'but orders must be obeyed. If they were not, I should be the one to get into trouble, and I do not wish to get into trouble. You say you haven't got the nerve? Perhaps we can remedy that.' He took from his pocket a round silver box rather like the powder cases that women carry in their handbags, and flipping back the hinged lid held it out invitingly across the table.

The man called Cornish took a step forward, and his twitching fingers shot out to grasp the object eagerly. Then he stopped suddenly and reluctantly drew his hand back. 'No, no,' he said thickly. 'I don't want any of that stuff. I won't have it. I promised — '

'Don't be foolish,' said Schwartz, still holding out the box temptingly. 'You need it, my dear fellow. Look at your hands and your lips. You're all in pieces. Promises are all very well, but it is absurd to refuse the medicine that cures you.'

Cornish hesitated, and then suddenly, with a little grunt, he snatched the box and, taking out a pinch of white powder, placed it on the back of his hand and sniffed it up his nostrils. He exhaled his breath slowly, and with enjoyment, like a man who had tasted his first cigarette after several days' abstinence. 'Ah, that's better!' he breathed, and would have returned the box of dope to Schwartz, but the fat man waved it away.

'Keep it,' he said. 'You will feel the need

of some more in an hour or two. Keep it.' Cornish closed the lid and slipped it into his pocket. Schwartz swayed his large face up and down approvingly. 'That's a sensible fellow,' he said. 'And now, about this Bond Street business. The boss wants a detailed plan of the bank, which, since you work there, should be easy for you to make.'

'Is that all he wants?' asked Cornish.

'Not quite all.' The fat man took an envelope from his pocket and flicked it across the table. 'On the twenty-first, which is Thursday of next week, you are, I believe, working on late duty?' He waited for a confirmatory nod. 'You are to make some excuse to remain behind after your fellow clerks have departed, and carry out the instructions you will find in that envelope. They are quite simple, and you will receive ample reward for your help.'

The potent drug was evidently taking effect on Cornish's brain, for he picked up the envelope with a laugh and ripped it open. Glancing at the contents, he nodded. 'I can do this,' he said, and his voice was no longer hesitant, but decisive.

'But I shall want paying well. I'm bound to be suspected, and I shall have to clear out of the country. I'm not taking that risk for nothing. I want halves.'

'That can be arranged,' agreed Schwartz. 'The labourer is worthy of his hire. You will get what you deserve.' There was a devilish whisper of evil in his voice, and Lowe, watching that overfed face, was convinced that after Cornish was no longer useful, he would receive little in the way of reward — a quick stab perhaps, or a bullet, but certainly nothing else.

Cornish was speaking again, and Lowe turned his attention to what he was saying. 'After I've done this for you, will you leave me alone?' he asked. 'Will you stop threatening me?'

'That is understood,' answered Schwartz. 'I have the boss's word that after you have carried out the instructions in that envelope, we shall trouble you no more. We shall help you to make your getaway, and then you will be free to do as you like. There are many places abroad where a man with money in his pocket can find enjoyment.'

'I hate being mixed up in it,' muttered Cornish, 'but I've no option in the matter. If I don't do as you want, I suppose that infernal cheque will reach the hands of my employers and I shall be arrested, anyway.'

'You put the matter crudely but correctly,' purred the fat man. 'And after all, you are being offered an opportunity. The pay of a bank clerk is not a fortune. You have the chance of making a fortune. It is not a chance that you would get every day.'

'And even if I succeed in getting out of the country, I shall be branded as a felon for the rest of my life,' retorted Cornish bitterly.

'You are that, anyway,' said Schwartz smoothly. 'Six months ago you forged a cheque for five hundred pounds, which you have managed to cover by falsifying your books. We have the proof of that in our possession. It is only a matter of time before the bank discovers what you have done. You can't keep it hidden much longer. It is better to be hanged for a sheep than a lamb.'

'It is better not to be hanged at all,' said Cornish. 'However, you seem to have got me in a pretty tight corner, and I've got to do as I'm told.' He buttoned up his overcoat. 'There's nothing else, I suppose? I can go now, can't I?'

Schwartz nodded. 'Yes, there is nothing more to say,' he grunted. 'You will report to the boss at the other place tomorrow night.'

Cornish moved towards the door, and Trevor Lowe hurried noiselessly back to the concealment of the storeroom. This weak young bank clerk appeared to have got himself completely in the clutches of the gang, and in order to avoid the consequences of some past misdemeanour was prepared to commit a further crime. From the little he had heard, the dramatist was able to give a fairly good guess at what that further crime was to consist of.

He saw the door open and Cornish come out, this time alone, and as he passed the door behind which Lowe was crouching a sudden idea was born in the dramatist's brain.

Why not try and get Cornish on his

side? The young man obviously hated the whole business; was only agreeing because he had no other choice. Probably, if he were talked to in the right way, he would come over to the side of the law and help to lay the entire gang by the heels. It was worth a trial, at any rate, and there was no time like the present.

Lowe cautiously left the harbour of the stockroom and crept after the hurrying figure of the bank clerk. Cornish had evidently been to the place many times before, for he seemed to know the way blindfolded. He doubled and twisted about among the piles of packing-cases and other debris, finding his way in the darkness without a sound.

Lowe followed as well as he could, and finally traced him to the bottom of a long spiral staircase that went circling away into the gloom overhead. He could hear Cornish's feet clamping on the iron treads, and went up after him silently. Cornish was breathing heavily as he neared the top. Drug excesses had weakened his constitution badly. There was a trapdoor of some sort at the head of the spiral stairs.

Lowe could see him pulling back the bolt in the light of a match he had struck.

Coming up behind him, the dramatist gripped him by the shoulder and pressed his other hand over his mouth. Cornish gave a startled grunt that would have been a cry but for Lowe's muffling hand over his mouth. The match dropped from his fingers and he nearly collapsed on the little platform. He tried to struggle feebly, but he was like putty in the dramatist's grasp.

'Be quiet!' hissed Lowe in his ear. 'I am from the Yard.' He thought this was the most effective thing he could say, and so it proved, for Cornish's struggles ceased, and Lowe went on: 'Listen! You're in a bad way, Cornish, and you know it. But it's up to you whether you save yourself or not. I've been listening outside the door downstairs ever since you arrived, and I know the whole of the situation. If you want to be sensible, I'll try and help you. Do you understand?'

Cornish nodded helplessly. He tried to speak, but his tongue had gone as dry as a piece of scorched leather.

'I'm offering you the only chance you're ever likely to get,' said Trevor Lowe grimly. 'If you come across and tell all you know, I'll do my best for you. Otherwise I'll have you inside a cell in less than an hour. You can choose which way you like.'

Cornish found an apology for a voice. 'Let's get out of here,' he croaked. 'I'll talk to you outside. If the others hear us — ' He stopped, and Lowe felt him shiver.

'Open that trapdoor then,' whispered the dramatist. He watched the dim white of the other's hands as he fumbled with the bolts. As the trapdoor rose, he gripped him by the arm. 'How does that open from the outside?' he demanded.

'You can't open it from the outside,' breathed Cornish. 'You have to ring the bell, and they come up from below and open it.'

'How do they get in themselves?' asked Lowe.

'There's another way — from the river. I don't know it, but I know there is.' He tried to pull his arm away. 'For God's sake, don't waste time. They'll be coming up in a minute to fasten the trap behind me, and then we shall be caught.' He stepped through the trap and Lowe followed him.

'Come on, this way,' whispered Cornish, and led the way along a dark and narrow passage. Lowe saw, as they passed an open door, that it ran parallel with the room he had explored previously, and from which the shaft of the broken lift emanated.

At a doorway through which the cool air of the night was blowing, Cornish paused. 'This leads out into the yard. We shall be pretty safe here. What do you want me to do?'

'Come clean on the whole game,' answered the dramatist. 'Tell all you know. In short, squeal. I'll see that you come to no harm. There is such a thing as an assisted passage for those who help the police and want to leave the country. That business of the cheque could also be arranged. Only, you've got to play square.'

Cornish considered for a fraction of a minute, then gripped Lowe's arm impulsively. 'I'll do it,' he said. 'I'll tell you all I know. Who the head of the bunch is I don't know, but I know most of their hide-outs and where they meet. I never wanted to go in with them at all. They forced me to by holding the business of that cheque over my head. I got in a hole by betting and — and other things. I'll come clean, and glad to.'

'That's the spirit,' said Trevor Lowe. 'Now, listen. I'm rather anxious to get the bunch downstairs. Will you take a note for me to the nearest police station?' Cornish assented. 'Right!' The dramatist whipped out an envelope and a pencil, scribbled a brief note and handed it to the other, together with his card. 'Cut along with that and give it to the sergeant in charge,' he said, 'and come round and see me at Portland Place in the morning.'

'I will. You can count on me.' Cornish held out his hand and Lowe gripped it.

'I'm going back down below,' said the dramatist. 'Hurry as quickly as you can.' He watched Cornish fade away into the darkness, and then turned and re-entered the passage.

Two steps he took, and then the whole

of that ramshackle building seemed to fall upon him. He slipped to his knees, groping blindly with outstretched hands, and was dimly conscious of a muffled laugh. Then a greater darkness than the darkness of the night swamped his senses like a sea of velvet.

15

Gang Murder!

Unaware of what had occurred in the disused warehouse he had just left, Cornish made his way across the rubble-strewn yard and through a narrow gate into the street. Turning to his right, he went hurriedly up the ill-lit and narrow thoroughfare; and as he went, a silent black shadow detached itself from the wall of shadows by the warehouse gate and followed noiselessly in his wake.

Fifteen yards in the rear, the sinister trailer crept along; and twice when Cornish turned to cast a frightened glance back over his shoulder, the street was empty. He felt happier than he had done for many a long day. At last there seemed a chance of regaining something of the position that weakness and bad companions had lost him. He felt that accepting Lowe's offer was his only chance of salvation. But fate decreed that the chance should come too late.

The narrow lane-like street ended in a broader crossroads, and three houses from the point of intersection that silent, trailing figure came up with the speed of an arrow. There was the silver glint of a knife-blade in the light and a shrill scream, and then the figure of the killer passed on, rapid and noiseless as the passage of a cloud across the moon — passed on and was gone.

Cornish fell where he stood, writhing in the gutter like a wounded animal, the hilt of the weapon that had pierced his heart sticking out from between his shoulder blades.

A window shot up overhead and a woman looked out, her eyes wide with terror. She saw the thing that lay still twitching half on and half off the pavement, and her own shrieks added to the sudden din of the night.

Screaming was the custom of the country in that locality. It drew attention to the fact that something was wrong, and it kept the screamer out of any possible entanglement. The instinct of self-preservation was the root cause of it, for the denizens of that district wanted the police round as quickly as possible when there were killers abroad, and that was the only time they wanted them.

Other windows rattled open. Old caretakers who lived in the attics over the gloomy warehouses added their babel, and the hoarse cry of 'Police — police!' went drifting away on the night air.

No one went near the thing in the gutter. That was no concern of theirs. They were getting a free show, and that was all that troubled them. People who got too near or tried to render assistance were required to give their names and addresses for such objectionable proceedings as inquests and magisterial hearings, and anything to do with the law was anathema along that section of the river. Apart from which, interference did not always end in the courts. Gangsters had long memories, and were apt to resent such kindly offices.

Thus, when running feet were heard and two policemen appeared flashing their lamps ahead of them, the tumult and the shouting died, the windows silently closed, faces were withdrawn, and the silence of the night settled back over the narrow little street.

Cornish was lying still and rigid, with a slight froth on his lips, his glassy eyes staring into the black sky, when the constables reached him. They looked down grimly at what had once been a living man, and the elder shook his head.

'Dead as mutton,' he said, and pointed to the hilt of the knife. 'Looks to me like gang work. There's been a lot of trouble round here lately.'

The other, a younger man, shivered slightly. 'They ain't like human beings in this neighbourhood,' he muttered. 'Animals, that's what they are — animals.'

They looked up and down the street. There was not a sound from anywhere. The tragedy was done and finished with. In sixty seconds it was begun and ended. Tragedies like this — grim little highlights that nickered in and out of the dull picture of East End life — happened without witnesses. The dead man had been thrown up out of the night, and the night had closed down dumbly upon him.

'Better run through his pockets,' grunted the elder policeman. 'Might be something there to identify him. Then you'd better phone the station, Frank, for an ambulance and a doctor — not that a doctor can do him much good, poor devil.'

He opened the coat and felt in the inside pockets, pulling out a handful of papers — one or two letters and some scribbled memoranda. 'Name's Cornish apparently,' he remarked. 'Jim Cornish, and his address is 14, Alerdyce Road, Kensington. Hm, better go and phone, Frank.'

The younger policeman crossed over to a darkened warehouse and thundered on the door. He knew there was a night watchman in that particular building, and he hammered away until it was obvious even to the watchman's stolid brain that he intended to stay there until he got an answer.

The man appeared grudgingly, and swore he hadn't heard a sound in the street for the last hour. The policeman knew he was lying, but he also knew how impossible it was to get anyone to bear witness against the gangs down there. He ordered the watchman to admit him to the little office, and in a few minutes he was through to his station.

'Got a murder job here, Sergeant,' he said. 'Fellow named Cornish. There was a knife in his back. Looks like a gang crime.'

'Right! Have you got help there?'

'Yes, 2033 is with me. He's searching the body now.'

'Where are you phoning from?' demanded the sergeant.

'A warehouse in Cotton Street.'

'Any witnesses?'

'Not a soul. The whole place here is as dead as the grave. Not a sound anywhere. The watchman here was awake, but he swears he never heard a sound. And we heard the screaming two streets away; but you know how it is — they'd cut their tongues out sooner than run foul of the gangs.'

The sergeant at the other end said something unprintable about the inhabitants of the district in general. 'Hang on there and I'll send the inspector and an ambulance.'

The constable hung up the receiver and went back to his colleague. He found him peering with interest at an envelope and a card.

'Look here, Frank, what I've just found in this fellow's pocket,' he said as the other joined him, and handed the card and the envelope to him.

The younger policeman looked at them and whistled. 'Jupiter!' he exclaimed. 'Trevor Lowe is in this business, is he? This chap must have been on his way to the station with this note when he was done in.'

'That's about it,' replied the other, 'and Trevor Lowe's still in that disused warehouse at the end of Cotton Street. You'd better take these straight along to the station, Frank, while I wait here.'

So engrossed were the two policemen that they failed to notice the sudden signs of activity that had taken place in the shadows of Cotton Street. Like black ghosts, figures were creeping towards them out of the darkness — stealthy sinister forms that moved like cats, silently and noiselessly on their rubber-shod feet.

Frank had turned away to carry out the other policeman's suggestion when with a sudden concerted rush, the murder band were on them.

'Look out!' shouted the elder constable, and his hand flew for his whistle; but it was struck from his grasp before it could reach his lips, and a sharp searing pain caught him under his left arm. The cry he tried to utter was drowned in a rush of blood that filled his throat, and he stumbled forward to his knees.

A confused mass of struggling figures filled the street for a few seconds, and then faded away into the shadows, leaving behind not one, but three motionless forms in the refuse-filled gutter. And with them went the note that Trevor Lowe had given to Cornish for delivery.

Truly the inhabitants of Cotton Street had been provided with a star show that night!

16

Trevor Lowe's Ordeal

How much time passed while he was in the shrouded blackness of unconsciousness, Lowe was unable to guess. That velvety, impenetrable darkness which had so suddenly overtaken him as he turned to re-enter the warehouse dissolved to a murky grey, accompanied by sharp, darting pains in his eyes and temples, and a vague sound as of rushing water. He opened his eyes, and a blaze of light sent such a spasm of pain through his head that he closed the lids again quickly to shut it out. The pain continued, however, throbbing and hammering through his brain until he felt sick with it. He was able now to distinguish that the sound he had taken for rushing water was the low, whispering voices of several men talking rapidly and excitedly. He waited for a few moments with closed eyes, and then, as the throbbing died down slightly, he ventured to open them again.

He could see nothing at first, for his senses were still unsteady and swimming. Then he discovered that the light came from the hurricane lantern on the table at which Schwartz had been sitting when he interviewed Cornish. Schwartz was still there, but he was no longer sitting. His place had been taken by a slimmer figure — a figure dressed in a long black coat with its head shrouded in a bag-like mask. Lowe felt his heart pulse with excitement. The newcomer was the king pippin of the outfit — the man who directed operations. The sudden extra pulsing of his heart sent a rush of blood to his head, and he almost fainted from the pain.

'Somebody has been careless,' he heard the cold voice with its slight American accent saying, as he recovered himself by a supreme effort of will. 'This infernal fellow must have followed one of you here. I don't know who he is, but he's disguised, and the sooner we get him out of the way the better. He's probably a law man of some sort. You're quite sure you settled Marlow before you left him?'

The last remark was addressed to two new arrivals who had come while Lowe was unconscious, and the bigger of the two nodded.

'That's all right, then,' continued the man in the mask. 'Marlow was a fool to think he wouldn't be closely watched.' The speaker turned slightly in his chair. 'It's lucky that you were able to prevent Cornish getting through with that note. It would have been disastrous.'

'I made short work of him,' grunted a thick-set man who was lounging against the wall, and whom Lowe recognised as the fellow he had followed from the Full-rigged Ship. 'I went up after him to fasten the trap, and heard this bloke here talking to him. I signalled the alarm down here, and after Mr. Schwartz had dealt with that — ' He jerked his head towards Lowe. ' — I went after Cornish. Some fool of a woman screamed, so I couldn't get the note then, but I roused up a few of the boys and made up for lost time later. There are two bloody flatties less in the force tonight, anyway.'

'You did very well, Slater; I shall see that you are rewarded,' said the masked man. 'The next question is, how are we going to dispose of this fellow?'

'Put a bullet through his head and sling him in the river,' suggested Slater, but the gang leader shook his head.

'No, just a moment — let me think.' He rested his elbow on the table and dropped his chin into his cupped hand.

So his note had not been delivered, thought Lowe, as he watched him, and his heart sank. He had been hoping that a few seconds would see the arrival of the help he had asked for, and the rounding up of everybody on the premises. Inwardly he criticised himself severely for not having taken more precautions when he had caught up and talked with Cornish. And what was that they'd said about Marlow? So he had been put on the spot as well. Lowe's hurried thoughts were interrupted.

'His presence here is a nuisance,' murmured the man in black. 'I had important business at the other place when your urgent message forced me to come here. I dislike having my plans upset, and those responsible must suffer. Is he conscious yet?'

Schwartz swung round, and in the nick of time Lowe closed his eyes and allowed himself to relax. He had been securely bound and gagged, and he thought that it would be useful to pretend to be still unconscious. No good could be served by letting these people know that he had recovered his senses and heard what they had been talking about. He felt Schwartz bend over him and peer into his face. Then he was gripped roughly by the shoulder and shaken.

'No; he's still dead to the world,' reported the fat man with a chuckle. 'I must have hit him harder than I thought.'

'Those rubber coshes are handy little weapons,' said the gang leader. 'Listen, I'll tell you what we'll do with him.' He leaned forward across the table. 'It's now low tide, and that cellar under the river entrance will be empty. We'll put him in there. It's flooded at high tide, and when the water goes down again we can cut his bonds, remove the gag, and let all that's left of him drift down the river.'

'I think it would be safer to stick a knife in his ribs — ' began Slater, but the other turned on him with a snarl.

'I'm not asking you what you think!' he rasped. 'I'm telling you what you're going to do.'

Slater shrugged his shoulders. 'Sorry,' he muttered. 'All right, carry on!'

'Pick him up,' ordered the masked man, and Schwartz and Slater came over to where Lowe was lying and stopped.

The dramatist decided that he would still play the unconscious game, though he couldn't for the moment see how it was going to help him. In fact, he didn't see how anything was going to help him. Helpless as he was if they carried out the gang leader's plan, nothing could save him from being drowned like a rat in a trap.

He had already surreptitiously tested the cords that secured his wrists and found them immovable. Whichever of the three had done the job had done it well, for the knots wouldn't give a fraction of an inch. However, Lowe had no intention of giving up hope while there was life; though as Schwartz and Slater slung him up between them, he had to confess to himself that there was very little likelihood that he would see another day.

'I'll light the way.' The masked man took a torch from his pocket and pressed the button. 'Come on, hurry up! I want to get away from here.'

He went over to the door and pushed it open. They carried Lowe through, and the gang leader led the way down the passage. At a point halfway along, he turned sharply into a branch passage that Lowe hadn't noticed before. It sloped downwards, and a chill breath of wind laden with the unmistakable smell of the river blew round his head. It was cool to his hot forehead, and soothed the burning of his brain. Presently they stopped before a heavy door in which was a perforated grating of rusty iron, and, taking a key from his pocket, the gang leader bent to the lock.

The door had evidently been used frequently, for the key turned without a sound. As the door was pulled open,

Lowe heard the sound of lapping water, and the wind blew more strongly. He caught sight of twinkling lights in front as he was carried across the threshold, and found that they had emerged into the open air onto a crazy landing stage.

'Put him down,' ordered the masked man, 'and come and help me open this trap.'

Schwartz and Slater dropped him without ceremony, and as he fell heavily Lowe made a further discovery that rather surprised him. The landing-stage was composed of stone. The others walked over to one corner, and he looked cautiously about him. So far as he could see in the darkness, the landing-stage was barely six feet wide — a narrow shelf that had been built onto the back of the warehouse. He had no time for a more thorough examination, for Schwartz and Slater came back panting.

They jerked him up and carried him over to where the masked man was directing a carefully shielded ray of light. Lowe saw through half-closed eyes that they had raised a heavy flagstone, and the light of the torch revealed a flight of worn and dirty stone steps leading down into the darkness. As Schwartz and Slater began to descend, a wave of evil-smelling air, stale and fetid, wafted up from the place.

'I'll follow with the torch,' said the gang leader in a low voice. 'Hurry up!'

They negotiated the steps, cursing as they slipped on the slime that filmed the stone, and presently reached the bottom. The trap led down to a low-ceilinged, cave-like cellar, the floor of which was already awash from the river that swirled through a rusty grating at the far end. Lowe wondered what the original object of the place could have been, and came to the conclusion that it had been a storehouse, and that the broad grating had been added after it had been built, though for what reason he couldn't imagine.

'Put him down there,' directed the man in black, pausing on the bottom step, and they dropped him with a splash into four inches of ice-cold water. 'Good! Now let's get away,' he continued. 'When the tide goes down, you can come back and remove the cords and the gag and raise that grating. If you push him out, the current will carry him downstream, and before he's found he'll be several miles away.'

He began to mount the steps while he was speaking, and the two gangsters followed him. Presently the dramatist heard the thud of the stone trap as it fell into place, and then there was silence except for the rhythmic lap-lap of the water.

He tried once again to loosen the cords at his wrists, but he only succeeded in drawing the knots tighter, and the fact that the thin rope soon became soaked through did not help matters. At the end of ten minutes he ceased his efforts and lay panting from his exertions.

He heard the melancholy hoot of a tug from somewhere beyond the grating, and the water round him rose and fell in waves with a squelchy splashing sound as the boat passed and its wash sent a broad ripple over the surface of the river outside.

It was a nasty position. He was as helpless as a newborn child, and though he racked his brains until his head ached he could find no way out. There was no doubt that the water was rising. It had barely reached the lobes of his ears when Schwartz and Slater had deposited him there, and now it was lapping round his chin. He tried to sit up, but the way in which he had been secured made it impossible.

No, there was no help for it. Nothing but a miracle could save him this time. He had managed on other occasions to escape by the skin of his teeth, but this was different.

And then, as G. K. Chesterton says they sometimes do, a miracle happened. There came a scraping sound from the direction of the head of the steps, and, twisting round, Lowe saw the trapdoor open, and a ray of light shot down into the darkness. It sprayed this way and that, and finally focused on his bound figure. It was only the gag that prevented him from giving vent to a cry of sheer amazement, for the holder of the torch was a woman!

17

The Mystery Woman

The newcomer gave a little exclamation as she saw him, and hurried down the remainder of the steps. Splashing through the water regardless of her silk-clad ankles, she bent over Lowe and fumbled at the knots at his wrists with a white, well-manicured hand. It cost her five minutes in time and a broken nail before she succeeded in loosening them.

'Perhaps you can untie the others yourself,' she said as she pulled off the gag. 'You'll probably make a quicker job of it than I will.' Her voice was low and pleasant, with the slightest trace of an American twang.

Lowe sat up with her aid and quickly freed his ankles. 'I don't know who you are,' he said with a smile as he rubbed vigorously at his cramped limbs to get the

185

circulation back, 'but you have certainly saved my life.'

'I guess that should be sufficient for you,' she replied. 'There is no reason why you should know who I am.'

He rose unsteadily to his feet and looked at her. She was of medium height, and he judged her age to be somewhere in the late thirties, though the light made any real hazard problematical. She might quite easily have been younger or older; it was difficult to tell. She was expensively dressed. The plain coat she was wearing had the elusive simplicity of Paris in every line.

'We may as well get out of this place,' she said with a shiver of disgust. 'That is, if you feel strong enough to walk.'

'I'm not only strong enough, but very glad to have the opportunity,' said Lowe. 'Until you put in such a timely appearance, I never thought I should be in a position to walk again.'

She made no reply, but led the way up the steps. The cool air of the night was very welcome to the dramatist after the bilge-water smell of that unpleasant cellar, and he drew great gulps of it into his lungs.

'Help me re-close this trap,' said his rescuer, and he lowered it gently by its iron ring. 'Now,' said the mystery woman, 'the best thing you can do is to go home to bed.'

'That is no doubt very good advice,' replied Lowe with a smile, 'but I have one more piece of work to do before I can take it.'

'What's that?' she asked.

'Without knowing exactly how you stand in relation to this gang of cut-throats,' he answered coolly, 'I don't think I can reply to that question.'

She was silent.

'What are *you* going to do?' asked Lowe after a slight pause.

'I'm going home,' she said shortly, and turned towards the dark bulk of the old warehouse.

Guided by the light of the torch she carried, they passed through its dusty, empty rooms and passages, finally emerging through a broken door into Cotton Street.

'I'll leave you here,' she said abruptly. 'The police station is only a few streets away. If you cross the road and take the first turning to the right at the top of this street, you'll come out nearly opposite to it.'

'What makes you think I want the police station?' asked the dramatist in surprise, for that was precisely where he had intended to go.

'You said you had a piece of work to do,' she replied. 'I wondered what you meant for a moment. It was rather stupid of me. Of course, you're going to arrange for the warehouse to be surrounded, so that when Schwartz and the other man come back to look for your body they'll walk into the hands of the police. You wouldn't tell me because you were afraid I might warn them. That's right, isn't it?'

'Quite right,' assented Lowe.

She laughed — a little hard laugh. 'You needn't have been afraid,' she said, and her voice was full of suppressed venom. 'I wouldn't raise a finger to save them all from hell!'

'Why, what have they done to you?' said the dramatist.

'*They* — nothing!' she answered. 'The man who controls them — everything. You're trying to get him, aren't you? You'll have to be quick if you want to get him before I do.'

'You know him.' It was a statement rather than a question.

'Oh yes, I know him!' She laughed again, and the sound was not pleasant. 'I know him very well. I'm seldom very far away from him. I've followed him most everywhere. I could have got him again and again, but I wasn't ready. Just to die would be too easy for him! I want him to suffer before the end as he's suffering now — wondering in his craven soul when the blow will fall, starting at every shadow in the night, and waiting for the past to rise up and strike him down.' She stopped suddenly. 'I'm talking too much,' she said. 'Good night!'

She would have turned away, but Lowe caught her by the arm. 'You have said either too much or too little. You know this man, and it's your duty to tell either the police or me who he is and where he can be found.'

189

'You can't force me to,' she replied quickly. 'What I have said, I have said to you without witnesses. I should deny it if I were confronted with the police.'

Lowe looked at her and shook his head. 'You are very foolish. If you have, as your words imply, some private scheme of vengeance against this man, you are worse than foolish. He is a murderer, and the law punishes murderers. Deliver him into the hands of the law and let it take its course.'

'No!' She almost shouted the word. 'Two years ago I made a vow, and I'm going to keep it.'

'You realise that it is my duty to detain you?' said Trevor Lowe.

'You mean have me arrested?'

He nodded, and she shrugged her shoulders. 'I realised the risk of that when I waited and released you from that cellar,' she replied. 'I took the risk. If you wish to take advantage of that, you must do so.'

Lowe removed his hand, which still rested on her arm. 'I'm not,' he retorted shortly. 'I owe you a debt for saving my

190

life. I always pay my debts if I can. Good night.'

'Good night — and thank you.'

She held out her hand and he took it. She had gone two yards when, impulsively, she came back. 'I'll tell you one thing,' she said a little breathlessly, 'though I don't think it will help you much. The man you are after is an American. His name is Al Brandt, though he doesn't call himself that in this country. Now go and find him, and if you're quick you may find him alive!'

She was gone before Lowe could reply, and he saw her slim figure disappearing into the shadows of Cotton Street. Trevor Lowe stared after her for nearly five minutes before he moved away, and his thoughts were chaotic when finally he made his way towards the police station.

At eight o'clock that morning, a white-faced and sullen-looking Schwartz, accompanied by a nerveless and whining Slater, was marched into the charge room of Deptford police station and formally charged with the attempted murder of Trevor Lowe.

They had returned to the warehouse half an hour before and walked into the arms of the men whom the dramatist had arranged to watch the place. And as they were led cursing and pleading to the cells to await being taken before the magistrate, the man who had brought about their arrest and whom they had expected to find dead was sleeping dreamlessly, utterly exhausted with his night's work.

18

Gregory Carr's Call

Trevor Lowe was up early the morning following his adventure at the warehouse in Cotton Street. Although he had slept for barely three hours, he looked as fresh and alert as usual by the time he had shaved and bathed and had his breakfast.

Big Ben was striking nine when he reached Westminster and passed in through the Whitehall entrance to New Scotland Yard. He was shown straight up to Shadgold's bare, cheerless office and found the inspector seated at his desk, laboriously writing a report.

Shadgold laid down his pen and looked up with a smile. 'Morning, Mr. Lowe,' he said. 'Very good of you to come round so early. I suppose Mr. White told you I waited as long as I could to see you last night.'

Trevor Lowe nodded. 'Yes,' he said. 'He

also told me about the Marlow affair. He says Marlow knew something.'

'He did,' said Shadgold gruffly, 'and he's taken his knowledge to the grave. I am pretty certain that it was connected with the identity of the head of this bunch of cut-throats. The whole business is a blessed jigsaw puzzle from beginning to end. What sort of luck did you have last night? As a matter of fact, when it got so late and you didn't show up, I nearly came down to the Full-rigged Ship myself!'

'You wouldn't have found me there,' smiled the dramatist. 'But, to answer your question. I've got two of the gang under arrest, and I've found the store of cocaine. Apart from that, I'm afraid very little.'

Shadgold opened his eyes. 'Well,' he remarked, 'that's something to be going on with! Tell me all about it.'

Lowe did so.

'Al Brandt, eh?' commented the burly inspector. 'Hm! So that's the fellow we're after, is it? Well, it doesn't help much. I've never heard of him.'

'The woman said he was an American, so that probably accounts for that,' said the dramatist. 'He may be quite a big bug in his own country.'

'I'll see if they know anything about him in Records,' said Shadgold, and pressed a bell. He scribbled a few lines on a sheet of paper and gave it to the messenger who answered the summons. 'Take this along to R.O.,' he ordered, and the man departed. 'They've got no end of people in the files that I've never heard of,' he continued, feeling in his pocket for one of the atrocious black cigars he was in the habit of poisoning the air with, and jamming it in the corner of his mouth. 'Perhaps they'll turn up something about Al — what's-his-name — Brandt.' He applied a match to one end of his cigar and blew out a cloud of evil-smelling smoke. 'Shame about those poor devils of policemen,' he went on, shaking his bullet head. 'It's a bad district down there at the best of times. What are they doing about this fellow Cornish? I suppose there'll be an inquest.'

'Naturally.' Lowe puffed hard at his

pipe. 'They told me at the station that nothing was found on him — not so much as a scrap of paper to show where he lived. Of course that can be traced through the bank where he was employed now they know his name. I was able to supply that information. These brutes killed him so that my message shouldn't reach the police, and they had to kill the constables for the same reason, since they had read it. Drastic move, but it saved the situation.'

Inspector Shadgold reached across for the ashtray. 'Seems as though that young fellow had all the earmarks of a thorough-going blackguard, the way he was out to cover up his past. A scamp like that wouldn't care how many crimes and murders were committed so long as he got away with his skin.'

'Oh, no, that's hardly fair, Shadgold,' said Lowe with a shake of his head. 'Cornish wasn't so deep-dyed as all that. His trouble was an exceptionally weak character, with what little willpower he possessed undermined by drugs. He wouldn't have had anything to do with that crowd unless he'd been forced, and chances are they would have killed him in any case after he'd served his purpose, in spite of rosy promises. There are thousands like him, Shadgold, all over the world, and they usually end up by falling prey to unscrupulous rogues who don't hesitate to throw them over afterwards.'

'It's a nasty business, anyhow,' grunted Shadgold. 'I shall be mightily pleased to get this fellow Brandt nice and snug in a condemned cell. He's responsible for all this wholesale slaughter. The average crook over here is a peaceful enough fellow, but of course if you fill him up with snow, there's no telling what he'll do.'

There was a slight pause, which was broken by Trevor Lowe. 'You know that the most interesting feature of this case is the two mysterious women who have cropped up. There's that woman at Gregory Carr's, for instance — '

'Nothing mysterious about her,' broke in Shadgold, 'except the quick way she went. By the way, I must get her name from Carr. She might be able to help us.'

'I've no doubt he'd be only too pleased

to give it to you — if he knew it,' answered the dramatist with a smile.

The cigar fell out of Shadgold's suddenly opened mouth and spattered sparks over his blotting-pad. 'If he — ' he began, and then explosively: 'But, good God, he must know the name of his own fiancée!'

'She wasn't his fiancée', said Lowe gently. 'He knows no more about her than we do, and that's nothing. She's just as mysterious as the lady who saved my life.'

'Then what did the young fool want to tell lies for?' demanded Shadgold, flushing. 'Hampering the ends of justice, that's what it is. Why, that woman might have been able to tell us everything we want to know.'

'Even you must have noticed that she was rather pretty,' said the dramatist, 'and Carr is young and therefore susceptible. I don't think you've got to go very deeply into the reason why he didn't give her away.'

'The fellow ought to be arrested,' growled the Scotland Yard man.

'Oh, come, you were young yourself

once!' said Trevor Lowe. 'Didn't they call you the 'answer to the housemaid's prayer' when you walked a beat?'

'I'd like to have heard anyone dare!' roared the inspector, his face a beautiful shade of purple. 'Who told you that, Mr. Lowe?'

'I forget now,' murmured the dramatist. 'However, to revert to this woman — I don't think she had anything to do with the gang, in spite of the fact that she was at the house at Oxshott on the night that young Carr stumbled into trouble.'

'Then what's she doing mixed up with the affair?' demanded Shadgold, relighting his cigar with an elaborate air of dignity.

'I haven't the faintest idea,' answered Lowe. 'What is the other woman doing mixed up in the affair?'

Shadgold had opened his mouth to reply when the messenger returned from the records department. He carried a thin folder, which he laid in front of the inspector. 'This is what you wanted, sir,' he said, and receiving a nod of dismissal, withdrew.

Shadgold flicked back the cover and

glared at the few slips of paper that were clipped inside. 'This is the man we're after,' he grunted, 'but it doesn't give us much information. Look for yourself.'

He pushed the file across the desk and Lowe bent over it. The details on the typed slips were meagre:

'AL BRANDT. Nationality: American. No other name known. Clever organiser and gang leader. Head of the Boxers, a gang of hold-up men and racketeers operating in Chicago. Has at least seven murders to his credit, but well in with police chiefs, so has eluded justice. Is said to have threatened more than once to come to London and start a gang on the same lines as Chicago. Carries firearms and is dangerous.' Underneath in red ink was written in a neat hand: 'Disappeared from Chicago after shooting a member of his own gang. No trace. November 2nd, 1928.'

On the second slip was a brief description of the man, which, as Lowe saw at a glance, might easily apply to at least ten percent of the male population of London. The third slip consisted of a long list of the crimes committed by the Boxers. Lastly, there was a letter from the Central Detective Bureau, New York, briefly stating that there was a possibility that 'Al Brandt may try to enter England. All trace of him has been lost on this side, and I should esteem it a favour, if you come across this man, if you will let me know at once.' It was signed, 'John K. Farnum, Captain, Central Police Headquarters, New York City.' That was all, and so far as it helped them it was nothing.

'He seems to be a particularly unpleasant specimen,' remarked Trevor Lowe as he closed the folder.

'We knew that before,' growled Shadgold, rubbing at his moustache. 'The question is, how are we going to find him? That description means nothing. It's like looking for one needle in a thousand haystacks.'

'Our only immediate chance is that one or both of those fellows they pulled in at the warehouse in Cotton Street will put up a squeal,' said Trevor Lowe, 'and I personally think that it's a remote one. Not that they'll squeak, but that they know anything worth squeaking about.'

'Which means that we are about where we started,' muttered the Scotland Yard man with a frown. 'Confound the whole damn business. It's putting years on me. Why couldn't this infernal man stay in his own country?'

'I should say there were many excellent reasons,' said the dramatist. 'What I should like to know is why my mysterious friend of the cellar is so anxious to get him. I should say that was one of the reasons, and a pretty strong one.'

They discussed ways and means of locating Al Brandt but without either being able to hit upon a feasible scheme. There was absolutely nothing to go upon — not the smallest clue that would put them on the track of the whereabouts of the elusive criminal.

The dramatist went back to Portland Place finally in a mood that White privately described as unfit for civilisation. He ate his lunch in silence and spent the afternoon alone in his study working. Apparently this occupation had done nothing to improve his temper, for when he emerged at tea-time and White ventured a remark, Lowe glared at him so ferociously that the secretary swallowed a gulp of scalding tea before he realised it was so hot, and nearly choked himself.

After tea he began rambling restlessly about the flat, smoking pipe after pipe, his brows drawn together, his lips compressed into a thin line. His utter inability to formulate any plan by which he could get on the trail of Al Brandt was fraying his nerves.

In the region of six o'clock, he resolutely put the whole thing out of his mind and, settling himself down in a chair with a book, tried to concentrate on its contents. It was useless expending mental energy in thinking in circles. Perhaps if he allowed his brain to rest, an idea would come. He fixed his attention on the printed pages and had so far succeeded that he was becoming interested in the author's arguments when the telephone bell shrilled out an incessant clamour.

'See who that is, White,' he said without raising his eyes from the book. 'Unless it's important, I'm out!'

White went over to the instrument and took off the receiver. 'This is Mr. Lowe's secretary speaking,' he said. 'Who is that?' There was a pause, and then: 'Oh, hang on a minute, will you?' White turned, putting his hand over the mouthpiece. 'It's Gregory Carr,' he whispered, 'and he wants to speak to you. Says it's urgent.'

Trevor Lowe, with a harassed look in his eyes, came over and took the receiver from White's hand. 'Hello, that you, Carr? This is Lowe here. Anything up?'

'Yes, something rather odd,' came back Gregory's distant and excited tones. 'Remember the scene in my flat when that wholesale skirmish took place and you came along just in time to prevent our being blown sky high?'

The dramatist smiled a little sternly. 'I remember.'

'Well, d'you recollect my telling you I plugged one of the fellows through the hand?'

'Yes, I recall everything in connection with the whole affair,' Lowe said quickly and perhaps a little impatiently. 'What about it?'

'I've seen him.' Gregory's voice was definitely excited now. 'And I followed him to a block of flats almost next door to my place. I'm positive it's the same man. His hand's bandaged up underneath an outsize in kid gloves, and he's just about the same build. In fact, I'm willing to bet my — '

'Where are you now?' cut in Lowe. 'Piccadilly call box? Well, I'm coming round to your flat straight away.' The dramatist banged down the receiver and hurried out of the room without replying to the amazed White's string of questions.

'Well of all ... ' muttered that indignant individual, scratching his head.

In less than three seconds Lowe was back again, climbing into his overcoat. 'I'm going round to Carr's,' he said, and before White had time to reply, was gone.

19

The Man with the Bandaged Hand

Trevor Lowe hailed a taxi and gave the driver Gregory's address. 'As quickly as you can,' he rapped, jumping in and slamming the door. The man obeyed with such unusual celerity that Gregory, when he opened the door of his flat and found the dramatist, was considerably surprised.

'That was pretty snappy,' he remarked. 'How on earth did you manage it?'

'I didn't,' answered Lowe, stepping in. 'An ordinary taxi driver was responsible for the miracle. I gathered while I was paying his fare that he was a one-time mechanic at Brooklands, which was where he got his taste for speed. Pity they aren't all like him. Now tell me all about this man you've seen.'

Gregory led the way into the sitting room and at once began his story. 'I was crossing Oxford Circus,' he said, 'when I spotted a fellow on the other side of the road heading down Regent Street. He attracted my attention because there seemed to be something familiar about him. He was tall and rather distinguished-looking, with a small grey beard, and he was walking quickly with one hand in his coat pocket and the other swinging by his side. As I watched him he took his hand out of his pocket, and I saw that he was wearing what looked like brand-new kid gloves. But the glove on his right hand was quite obviously several sizes too large and being worn to hide a bandage. I could just see the top of the white stuff where his coat sleeve had rucked up.'

'Did he see you?' asked Lowe.

Gregory shook his head. 'I'm positive he didn't. I was one of a crowd charging across from one side to the other, and though he looked in my direction I'm certain he didn't see me.'

'I presume,' said the dramatist, 'it was the gloved hand that made you suspicious?'

'Exactly,' agreed Gregory. 'The moment I spotted that hand I knew why its owner had caught my attention. The fellow may have worn a silk scarf over his face when he came here, but he couldn't disguise his build, and it was that that first got me — then the stiff, obviously bandaged hand on top of that, and I was absolutely dead certain it was the mysterious gentleman who wanted to give me a free passport to heaven.'

'Let us hope it *would* have been heaven,' said Trevor Lowe. 'What did you do?'

Gregory Carr grinned. 'I followed him. A detective would probably think it pretty poor shadowing, but anyway, I managed to keep up, and he didn't look round once until he reached Piccadilly, where he just shot a casual glance backwards before crossing the road. He didn't see me. It was there that I thought I'd mucked up the whole thing. Before I could get across the road myself, a stream of cars, buses and things most inconveniently blocked my vision, so that when I did eventually reach the other side of the road I'd completely lost all trace of the gentleman with the beard.'

'Hard luck,' murmured the dramatist. 'Did you find him again?'

'Only by a sheer fluke,' continued Gregory. 'It's always less crowded in the road when people are crossing than on the pavement, and I saw him again a few seconds later dodging over to Lower Regent Street. I took darn good care not to let him slip again, and stuck to his heels till he went into a block of flats in Merriman Street; it runs through to the Haymarket from Lower Regent Street — '

'I know Merriman Street well,' said Lowe, rising. 'What was the address?'

'It's the last building but one on the right-hand side, Haymarket end,' explained Gregory. 'Look here,' he added, 'if you're thinking of going along now, I'll come and show you!'

'No, I'd rather you didn't, if you don't mind,' said the dramatist. 'You've already done enough, and I shan't experience any difficulty in finding the place you described. I know that district well.'

Gregory followed Lowe to the door. 'Do you think you're likely to get anything out of it?' he asked anxiously. 'Queer, you know, the fellow hanging out almost on my doorstep.'

'That was probably a coincidence,' said the dramatist as he grasped Gregory's hand. 'In fact, it may all be a coincidence. This grey-bearded man may be quite a harmless individual after all. I'm certainly going to have a look round all the same.'

He left Gregory feeling rather dejected and fed up. The excitement of his recent shadowing expedition had made him forget his own troubles, but now that he had told the dramatist everything, the world somehow automatically resumed its normal gloomy outlook and seemed suddenly to be devoid of all interest. With a grunt he turned back to the sitting room and started scanning the advertisement columns of the daily newspapers in the hope of spotting a likely job.

Trevor Lowe, on the other hand, was no longer depressed or irritable. Less than an hour ago he had been down in a fit of depression, and not altogether without reason, considering what he had already achieved. He had wished Al Brandt and his scandalous crew in a place where even asbestos suits wouldn't be sufficient to keep off heat, because he had found himself suddenly confronted by a blank wall which refused most obstinately to be scaled, and Lowe didn't like walls of that kind.

But now, as he made his way thoughtfully in the direction of Merriman Street, he was once more his normal self, and the person responsible for the lightning change was Gregory Carr. There was food for thought in Gregory's story, but the main point that occurred to Lowe's mind again and again as he strode along was a connecting link with his own adventures in the Cotton Street warehouse. The man in the mask! He had had a bandaged hand and fitted Gregory's description perfectly — that was, with the exception of his face; Lowe had not been able to see that. Was it possible that he was on the trail of this man now — and was he Al Brandt?

Before he reached Merriman Street, he had decided on his plan of campaign. The situation was a delicate one. Under no circumstances would it do to let this man with the grey beard know that anyone had been enquiring about him, and, therefore, Lowe decided to adopt a plan that he had thought out.

As he neared the block of flats to which Gregory had followed his quarry, he loosened his tie slightly and pushed his hat over one eye at a rakish angle. His brisk walk changed to an uncertain stagger and his gait became rather unsteady. The flats were housed in a tall sheer building of white stone, and the dramatist estimated that it must contain anything between twenty and thirty suites which in this exclusive and central locality would produce for the owner a rental figure running well into five figures.

A broad flight of marble steps led up to the entrance which had been fitted with massive glass-panelled swing doors. Lowe stumbled up the steps with difficulty, lurched against the doors and staggered through into the spacious hall beyond. From the ceiling at regular intervals, electric bowls threw down a mellow flood of white light onto the tiled floor. At the end of this rather ornate vestibule was a lift apparently operated by the spruce lad in a green and gold uniform who was, at that moment, seated in a chair nearby with his brilliantined head buried in a book.

As Trevor Lowe approached erratically, the boy jumped up and hastily put the book on one side. Making no attempt to speak to him or enter the lift, Lowe gazed round blankly at the walls as though he was rather puzzled to find them there at all. After a moment or two he turned to the boy and smiled uncertainly. 'Where'sh the — in'icator? Jolly ol' in'icator.' He swayed gently backwards and forwards. 'Mus' find in'icator. Wha'sh use buil'ing without in'icator?'

'Sorry, sir. There's no indicator here,' said the boy solemnly.

'Then there ough' to be,' said Lowe, wagging an admonitory finger in the boy's face. 'Don't you lem'me come here again without finding one. It's dish-dishgraceful. How's a feller to find a feller when he doesn't know who the feller is. Answer me that.'

'I couldn't say, sir,' said the lad,

suppressing a grin.

'Can't answer simple question,' mumbled Lowe. 'Not without in'icator. Feller I want may be in one flat, may be in another flat. May be in all the flats. Can't tell without in'icator.'

'Perhaps, sir,' said the liftboy, 'I can help you if you tell me what the gentleman's like.'

'Tha'sh a good idea,' said Lowe thickly. 'Very good idea. He'sh — a tall feller. Rather thin, with a grey beard.'

The liftboy frowned. 'That sounds like Mr. Anstruther, sir,' volunteered the boy after a moment's thought. 'Number fourteen, second floor. He went out though about half an hour ago.'

Lowe shook his head stupidly. 'Tha'sh not the name,' he grunted. 'Not the name at all. Not a bit like it. Mus' have made a mistake.'

'Mr. Anstruther is the only gentleman living here with a beard, sir,' said the boy.

'Extraordinary,' muttered Lowe. 'Most extraordinary. This is Royal Buildings, isn't it?'

'No, sir,' said the boy. 'This is Grayden

House; Royal Buildings is in the next street.'

'Made a mishtake. Shilly of me,' said the dramatist incoherently, feeling in his pockets and producing a shilling. 'Shtupid thing to make mishtakes. Never mind — try again. Keep on trying again till I find the feller I want.' He pressed the coin into the willing hand of the liftboy and, leaving that individual grinning all over his chubby face, made his way out through the swing doors.

Halfway along Merriman Street his walk resumed its normal steadiness, and he quickly readjusted his hat and tie. He had learned what he wanted to know. The man Gregory had followed was called Anstruther, and he lived in flat fourteen, Grayden House. The task now was to establish a connection between Mr. Anstruther of Grayden House and Al Brandt, late of the United States of America — and that was not going to be quite as easy!

20

The Blotting-pad Clue

The moment Trevor Lowe reached Piccadilly, he hailed a taxi and drove straight to New Scotland Yard, where he had the satisfaction of learning that Inspector Shadgold was working late. He was taken up and found the burly inspector labouring over a great sheaf of papers that he hadn't had time to wade through for the past fortnight. As Lowe entered, he put them to one side and glanced up curiously. 'What the devil has brought you here again?' he grunted.

Lowe pulled up a chair on the opposite side of Shadgold's desk and related first Gregory's story of the man with the bandaged hand, and then his own expedition to the block of flats in Merriman Street.

'Sounds interesting, damned if it doesn't,' admitted Shadgold. 'Good God, if it turns out to be Brandt we've just about come to the last chapter.'

'If it turns out to be Brandt,' said Lowe. 'That's what we've got to prove, and it's going to be difficult. We've got absolutely no evidence with which to arrest the man, so whatever our suspicions may be, we can do nothing, absolutely nothing, until we've got definite proof.'

Shadgold drummed on the desk with his fingers. 'That's perfectly true,' he said, frowning. 'Have you any suggestion to make?'

'Only that a close watch should be kept on Anstruther,' replied Lowe. 'That's the only thing I can suggest at the moment. Though it wouldn't hold good in a court of law, we have got one clue that rather tends to confirm our suspicions regarding Anstruther being the man we're after.'

The Scotland Yard man looked at him quickly. 'What's that?' he asked.

'The clue that Marlow left on the blotting-pad,' said the dramatist.

Shadgold started. 'By Jove! I had forgotten that,' he exclaimed. 'Of course

— the 'A' might stand for the initial letter of Anstruther. That's what you mean, isn't it?'

'Yes,' said Lowe. 'I don't think it is at all improbable. Unfortunately, we require something more than a probability, and that's one of the reasons I've come here tonight. First of all, I want you to arrange to have a close watch kept on this man Anstruther, and secondly I want to know if you've found out anything further about Marlow.'

Shadgold shook his head. 'Nothing of importance,' he growled, 'beyond the fact that he had apparently been swindling the income tax people for the past ten years. Whoever sent that threatening note to him seems to have been dead right on that score.'

'Now, that is an interesting point,' said Lowe quickly. 'Brandt — I think we can take it that he was the one who wrote to Marlow — must have been very familiar with Marlow's affairs to know that he was defrauding the tax people. I mean that normally the man would have kept it as private as possible.'

'Well?' grunted Shadgold.

'Well,' Lowe went on, 'doesn't it rather indicate that Brandt and Marlow might somehow or other have been on a friendly footing at one time? That would account for the information Marlow had up his sleeve and was willing to tell me. He knew Brandt was Anstruther, and was ready to give him away when they quarrelled.'

'I should think that was pretty near the truth of it,' murmured Shadgold, rubbing at his toothbrush moustache. 'It's good reasoning, anyway. Now I see why you want some further information concerning Marlow's affairs. You think that if we dig deep enough we might strike Brandt, otherwise Anstruther?'

The dramatist nodded slowly. 'At least it's a possible line to go on,' he answered.

'I'll show you all the stuff we've managed to collect.' Shadgold pressed a bell on his desk. 'It isn't much, but perhaps you may be able to find something in it.' He barked an order to the messenger who answered the ring, and the man went away, to return after a short interval with a file which he placed

219

in front of Shadgold before withdrawing again.

'Here you are,' said the burly inspector, pushing it towards Lowe. 'You can look for yourself. It's all typewritten with marginal notes. You'll find it quite easy to follow.'

For half an hour, Trevor Lowe busied himself scanning the contents. Suddenly he looked up, his finger on a certain passage. 'Did you notice this?' he asked.

Shadgold came to his side and, leaning over the dramatist's shoulder, let his eyes follow Lowe's moving finger as it ran over sentence by sentence of the short paragraph which had interested him. It was only a few lines to the effect that early in the summer of 1929 Marlow had paid a visit to America and stayed there for six months. His destination had been Chicago, and he had repeated his visit twice since that date.

'Now,' said Lowe, 'what exactly was Marlow doing in Chicago? It isn't the sort of place one would go to for a holiday, and his business interests don't appear to have ever necessitated his moving out of

England. He may have gone there the first time purely from a commercial point of view, but whatever the reason was, I'm willing to bet that it was in Chicago that he first met Brandt.'

Shadgold blew his nose loudly. 'I'm not disagreeing with you,' he remarked, 'but how is all this going to help?'

Trevor Lowe put down the folder and felt in his pocket for his pipe. 'If we can establish a connection between Brandt and Marlow,' he said, 'there is a possibility that we may be able to establish a connection between Brandt and Anstruther. After that, it won't be so difficult to associate him with this gang business.'

'But we know already that Brandt is the head of the gang,' interrupted Shadgold. 'That woman told us so herself.'

'That's quite right,' said the dramatist, 'but you know it's not evidence. You can't accuse a man merely on a woman's word. Especially when the woman won't come forward.'

The burly inspector snorted. 'Damn it all,' he growled irritably, 'doesn't matter which way you turn in this business; you always find yourself up against a brick wall.'

'There are more ways than one of dealing with a brick wall,' retorted Lowe. 'One way is to charge at it blindly, which is likely to do more damage to yourself than to the wall. The other, and the best way, is to remove it brick by brick. It takes longer, but it's the surest way in the end. I think in this case the brick-by-brick method is going to prove the best.'

Curiously enough, the same idea had occurred to Al Brandt.

21

Al Brandt's Idea

At almost exactly the same time that Trevor Lowe was discussing Al Brandt with Detective-Inspector Shadgold in the latter's office at Scotland Yard, Al Brandt was discussing Trevor Lowe in the bare and dimly lighted room of an empty house in Maida Vale. The door of the room was closed and the windows at either end carefully shrouded so that not even the miserable light of the single candle which provided the only illumination could penetrate beyond.

Standing with his back to the fireplace was the man whom Lowe had seen in the warehouse at Cotton Street, his features concealed by the silken mask which covered his face and chin and was tucked under the collar of the long, dark overcoat which he was wearing. Half a dozen men were grouped around him; men whose furtive expressions plainly showed the uneasiness that was troubling their minds. The man in the mask was speaking in the same low, toneless voice that he usually adopted.

'I know what you're all thinking,' he said, glancing from one to the other. 'You're thinking that things are not going exactly as I led you to believe they would. Well, to a certain extent you're right. But although we've had a good deal of bad luck, you must admit that we've had the other kind as well. We have succeeded in amassing a large amount of money, and we have not finished yet. We must overcome the danger which is threatening us by some means or other. It would be foolish to throw in the towel at the first setback.' He paused to see the effect of his words, and a thin weedy man with a discontented face thrust it aggressively forward and removed the half-smoked cigarette that drooped from the corner of his mouth.

'We've no intention of throwing in the towel,' he grunted, 'so long as there's not too much danger. But you've got to admit that if things go on like this, we shall all be in the soup. We can't use the 'ouse in Oxshott any more. The place at Cotton Street has been discovered. All the snow's been collared, and the cops have got Schwartz.'

'There's no need to go through all that,' cut in the other impatiently. 'The reason I've called you here tonight is to discuss a plan that will rid us of our most pressing danger and enable us to carry on.'

'Let's 'ear it,' said one of the men, and there was a murmur of agreement from the others.

'You shall,' replied the masked man. 'Our most pressing danger, as you will all agree, is this interfering amateur Lowe. He's at the root of all our trouble, and if once we can dispose of him our worries in the future will be negligible. How he managed to escape from Cotton Street the other night I don't know, and it doesn't matter much. All that concerns us is that he did escape. Therefore, before we think about anything else, we have got to evolve a method for getting rid of him once and for all. Do you all agree with me?'

'I agree with you, but it's easier said than done,' said the little thin man who had spoken before.

'I am perfectly aware of that,' replied the man in the mask. 'But I have a plan which I think will be effective. Listen!' He paused for a moment, and then clearly and rapidly began to outline his scheme. For ten minutes he went on, hardly stopping except to answer a few odd questions, and when he had finished his audience uttered little comments.

'Now that *is* a good idea,' admitted the thin man, and the corners of his slit of a mouth twisted into an unpleasant smile.

'I'm glad it appeals to you,' sneered the masked man. 'There's no reason why we shouldn't get busy and put it into practice immediately. The only way in a case like this is to deal with each obstacle as it arises, and deal with it thoroughly. Now there is one other thing I want to mention. We cannot use this place again — it would be too risky, so we have got to decide where we can hold our next meeting. At the moment we don't know to what extent, if any, the police are aware of the place at Vauxhall. If they don't know of its existence, then all well and good, we can continue to use that; but we shall have to make quite certain first. Some of you had better have a look round.'

He stopped speaking, and there was a moment's silence.

'I think that's all,' he went on presently. 'With regard to this plan for the removal of Trevor Lowe, I will arrange with the woman. Farson and Brice — ' He nodded towards the men who bore the names he mentioned. ' — can attend to the other details. The whole thing must go without a hitch. We cannot afford to make a mistake.'

For a further half hour they discussed and argued about the scheme the masked man had proposed, and when everything had been settled the meeting broke up. They left one at a time, and stole out by the back entrance of the house, making their way across the barren stretch of neglected garden, passing through one of the many apertures in the dilapidated fence into the road beyond.

As usual, the man in the mask was the

last to go. When no longer wearing the silken covering to his face, he stepped stealthily through the fence at the bottom of the garden and began making his way in the direction of the Edgware Road, his lips curved in a satisfied smile. He had succeeded in regaining the confidence of his associates; a confidence that had waned almost to breaking point. The complete obliteration of Trevor Lowe would leave them free to begin operations again.

Altogether his evening's work had been profitable, but in spite of that Al Brandt felt uneasy. Trevor Lowe, the police, and that other, more elusive danger hung over him; a danger which he found utterly beyond his power to grapple with.

As he walked rapidly along the silent street, his strained nerves started involuntarily at every shadow, and the slightest sound other than his own footsteps caused him to throw quick, furtive glances over his shoulder; for he was a man whom the fear of death had filled with endless doubts and fancies.

22

The Message

'Excuse me, sir,' said Trevor Lowe's housekeeper, putting her head round the door of the study. 'There's a man asking to see you. A Mr. Jelf. He says it's very urgent.'

The dramatist looked round from his desk and frowned. 'Jelf — Jelf,' he repeated. 'I've heard the name before somewhere.' He shook his head. 'I can't remember where though. Ask him to come in.' He glanced at the clock as the housekeeper withdrew and saw that it was just after eleven o'clock.

The man who was presently ushered in was a small and very nervous-looking individual who stood just inside the doorway and twisted the brim of his bowler hat undecidedly.

'Sit down, Mr. Jelf,' said the dramatist. 'I seem to know your name. What do you wish to see me about?'

Mr. Jelf's rather rat-like face showed signs of uneasiness. 'Know me name, do you, sir?' he stammered. 'The police haven't been looking for me, have they? Because I haven't had nothin' to do with it.'

'To do with what?' enquired Trevor Lowe in astonishment.

'Why, the murder of Mr. Marlow, of course,' muttered the man, and the dramatist gave an exclamation.

'Now I understand,' he said. 'Of course! You used to be Marlow's valet. You disappeared on the night he was killed.'

'That's right, sir,' admitted the other, nodding his head unhappily. 'But I didn't have nothin' to do with it. He was going to leave the country, and he paid me off that evening and told me he wouldn't want me no more.'

'Nobody ever suspected that you knew anything about it, Jelf,' said the dramatist. 'Mr. Marlow was killed at the instigation of a gang who sent him a threatening letter demanding money. As a matter of fact, the police *have* been looking for you, but only because they hoped you would be able to tell them something about your late master's affairs. But never mind that. Why have you come here tonight?'

'Cause I'm all sort of 'ot and bothered,' said Mr. Jelf wriggling nervously in his chair. 'When I said jest now I didn't know nothin', it wasn't quite true. I do know somethin', but I don't want to go to them police about it. I thought it would be better if I came to you, seeing as how you're a kind of private gentleman like, if you follow me.'

Trevor Lowe acknowledged what was probably meant to be a compliment and offered the man a cigarette to calm his nerves. 'Well, then, let me hear what you know,' he said, applying a lighted match to the end of the cigarette that Mr. Jelf was holding between unsteady fingers. 'Now take your time — there's no hurry.'

Mr. Jelf gave several jerky puffs and then fixed his pale, watery eyes on Lowe. 'Mr. Marlow engaged me back in the summer,' he began, 'when I was down and out, and would have taken almost anything. I'm not saying the job wasn't a good one. It was all right, and the money was regular, and I was pretty comfortable-like — even though he was difficult to please at times and let me 'ave a bit of 'is temper.' He shook his grease-plastered head, and then continued: 'However, that bit ain't got nothin' to do with what I wants to get off me chest. One day Mr. Marlow brought a man back with 'im: a well-dressed, tallish sort of cove with a beard.'

'What was his name?' interrupted Trevor Lowe quickly.

'Don't know 'is name,' replied Mr. Jelf. 'Never 'eard it mentioned. But they come in together, and it seemed to me as 'ow there was somethin' funny between 'em.' He wrinkled his small forehead. 'It was as if they were friends and not friends, if yer follow me.'

Lowe nodded. 'I understand,' he said. 'Go on.'

'Well, Mr. Marlow give this 'ere feller a drink,' went on Mr. Jelf, 'and then he spotted me in the background and told me to get out. I was going into the next room, but Mr. Marlow called me back and told me he didn't want me there at all. Told

232

me to clear out of the flat. Snappy about it, he was, too. I didn't like being spoken to like that, 'specially in front of strangers, so although I pretended to do what I was told I didn't go very far, if you follow me.'

'I follow you,' said Lowe mildly. 'You just went outside and listened at the keyhole, eh?'

Mr. Jelf started. "Ow did yer know?' he asked nervously.

'Because it's the natural thing you would do,' said the dramatist.

'Well, yer quite right, sir,' said the little man. 'That's what I did do, though I hadn't never done such a thin' before.'

'No, of course not,' said Lowe without a great deal of conviction. 'Well, what did you hear?'

'Not very much,' replied Mr. Jelf. 'They was talking very low, but I managed to catch a word here and there. There was some talk of America, and from what I did 'ear it seemed as though the two of 'em had met on the other side of the water, and that Mr. Marlow had recognised this other feller that afternoon in London. The feller with the beard sounded as if 'e was annoyed, and there was a few 'igh words, and I 'ear 'im say: 'Well, you better pay up and keep your mouth shut, or you're for it.' They weren't exactly the words he used, but that's as near as I can remember. One of them started walking about then, and I got a bit nervous in case Mr. Marlow should spot me listening, so I made myself scarce, if yer follow me.'

'Didn't you hear any more of the conversation at all?' asked Trevor Lowe. 'Didn't they mention when and where they had met in America?'

'No, sir,' said Mr. Jelf. 'I only heard that they'd done some sort of business together out there.'

'And you didn't hear the other man's name?' persisted the dramatist.

'No, sir, I didn't,' replied the little man.

'Pity,' muttered Lowe. 'Go on, tell me what else happened.

'That was all, sir,' said Mr. Jelf. 'There weren't nothin' else, until the other day Mr. Marlow told me to pack his things as he was going away. I thought he was going to take me with him, but instead he gave me one month's money and told me to clear out. And that was the last I saw of 'im until I read what 'ad happened in the papers. I'd have come forward before, only I felt too scared.'

'That was foolish of you,' said the dramatist. 'You should have told the police at once what you have just told me.' He rose to his feet. 'However, we can rectify your mistake. I'll take you down to Scotland Yard with me and you can repeat your statement to Detective-Inspector Shadgold.'

Mr. Jelf got up with remarkable celerity. 'I ain't going there,' he said. 'I ain't going there to 'ave them working off any of their third degrees on me. Oh, no!'

'Don't be stupid,' said Lowe sharply. 'You've got absolutely nothing to fear, and it's essential that you should come and make a signed statement. I'll go and fetch my hat and coat. I shan't be long.'

He left the study and went into his bedroom, but when he returned the room was empty. The terrors of Scotland Yard had apparently proved too much for Mr. Jelf's courage. Taking advantage of the dramatist's absence, he had, like the Arabs, folded his tent and stolen away.

Lowe clicked his teeth with annoyance. However, the man could not have gone far, so after a hasty glance round he hurried down the stairs to the front door. It was half open, and Lowe went out onto the step and looked up and down Portland Place in the hope of catching sight of the scared Mr. Jelf. But there was no sign of him, and Lowe was just turning to re-enter the house when he saw White coming towards him.

'What's the matter?' asked his secretary as he reached Lowe's side. 'You look annoyed about something.'

The dramatist explained. 'And now he's gone,' he said. 'The one person who could have possibly identified Anstruther as the man who had had suspicious dealings with Marlow. Taken fright like a scared rabbit.' He paused for a moment, biting his lip and frowning. Then suddenly making up his mind, he went on: 'You run upstairs and get on the phone to Shadgold. Tell him what's happened and ask him to send out a 'hurry' call to all stations and have Jelf pulled in. Meanwhile, I'll have a look round and see if I can see him anywhere.'

White disappeared upstairs, and the dramatist, closing the front door, began to walk down Portland Place towards Regent Street. A big saloon car that had been standing by the side of the kerb moved forward slowly and then, increasing its speed, shot past Lowe and came to a standstill a few yards in front of him.

The window was lowered and the face of a woman appeared. 'Mr. Lowe,' she called softly as the dramatist drew level, and he stopped in surprise. 'You are Mr. Trevor Lowe, aren't you?' she went on in a low, clear voice that held a tremor of excitement. 'I was introduced to you at the first night of *Caged Birds*. I hope you'll forgive my stopping you, but I was just going to call.'

'I'm afraid I don't remember you,' replied the dramatist. 'What did you wish to see me about?'

The woman glanced nervously up the street and drew back slightly. 'I want to ask your advice,' she whispered. 'I am in danger — great danger!' Her voice broke in a little sob, and Lowe took a step nearer.

'I'm afraid — ' he began, but she cut

him short with an impulsive little gesture of her gloved hands.

'Please listen to me,' she pleaded. 'If you will get into the car, I will explain everything — but do, please, be quick. I'm sure I am being followed.' She held open the door invitingly.

After a momentary hesitation, Lowe shrugged his shoulders and got in, and the door closed behind him with a snap. The woman removed a large bunch of flowers from the seat to make room, and, leaning forward, tapped on the front window as a signal to the chauffeur. The car moved forward, and Lowe sank back beside his companion, glancing covertly at her as he did so.

She was expensively dressed in black, and wore a short veil that hung like a thin mist in front of her dark, wide-set eyes. There was more than a trace of Latin blood in the pale beauty of her face, and the diamonds glittering on her fingers when she removed her glove he judged to be worth a small fortune.

He waited for her to speak, and presently she did so, turning slightly towards him. 'You must forgive me for this unconventional way of approaching you,' she faltered, 'but if you knew how frightened I am you would understand.'

'I think the best thing you can do,' he murmured, 'is to tell me exactly what the trouble is, and if I can help you I will.'

'Thank you,' she said. 'Well, it may sound ridiculous, but I'm afraid of being — of being kidnapped! For the last few days I have been followed everywhere, and last night somebody attempted to break into my flat.' Her voice was so low that it was scarcely audible, and she twisted her gloves this way and that between her fingers.

'Why come to me?' asked the dramatist. 'Why not go to the police and ask for their protection?'

There was a moment's silence, then: 'I can't do that,' she murmured. 'There would be such a scandal. You see, if I'm right, I think these people are working at the instigation of my husband. I know you are interested in these things, Mr. Lowe. You have on more than one occasion helped the police — ' She stopped suddenly, glanced quickly through the oval aperture at the back of the car, and then shrank into the corner with a little cry of dismay. 'Look, there!' she said. 'That car — '

Lowe looked and saw a few yards behind them the long radiator of another car following in their wake. 'Is that the car you've seen following you before?' he asked.

She nodded, and the pallor of her face increased. Her head began to slip gently sideways.

'I believe — I'm going — to faint,' she whispered. 'Give me the smelling salts — my bag.'

Slightly alarmed, Lowe seized the bag and fumbled among its contents. He found a small cut-glass bottle, which he uncorked and held beneath her shapely nose. The pungent salts seemed to revive her, for after a little while she sat up and looked at him with a smile.

'Thank you,' she said. 'Now would you mind very much if, before explaining any further, I waited until we reached my flat?'

'Not at all,' he replied, 'if you'd prefer it.'

He glanced again through the back window, and in spite of the fact that they had left the main road and were now passing through a side street, the car behind was following.

At that moment the chauffeur swung round to the right and increased his speed. The swaying motion of cornering caused the bunch of flowers on the woman's lap to slide off on to the floor, and Lowe, stooping, picked them up.

'Thank you,' she said as she took them. 'Aren't they lovely, Mr. Lowe? I am terribly fond of flowers.' She buried her face in the blooms. 'There's something so fresh about them, I think.' She held them towards him, and Lowe, politely doing what was obviously expected of him, leaned forward and smelled them.

As he did so, the bunch was thrust full into his face, and from somewhere concealed in its midst a jet sprayed a sweet, sickly, overpowering vapour into his nostrils and mouth. With a choking gasp, he struck the deadly flowers wildly from him and attempted to struggle to his feet. For a moment he was conscious of a smiling face and dark smouldering eyes, and then everything vanished into a misty uncertainty, and he collapsed in a huddled heap to the floor of the fast-moving car.

23

The Furnace

The car containing Trevor Lowe's limp and apparently lifeless body came to a standstill in the quiet side-turning within five seconds of his becoming unconscious, and almost immediately the other car that had been following drew alongside and two men jumped out. One of them pulled the door of the car open for the woman to alight, glanced at the dramatist's huddled figure, and grinned.

'Worked all right, eh?' he said quickly.

The woman drew the coat she was wearing tightly about her and spoke quickly. 'Of course it worked all right,' she snapped. 'And now I want to get away. What about the money?'

'The boss'll arrange with you about that,' said the man. 'You needn't worry, you'll do well out of this.'

The other man, a small but thick-set

individual with an ugly scar under his right eye, glanced up and down the road anxiously. 'Come on,' he growled impatiently. 'Don't let's stick around here — it's dangerous.'

The woman shrugged her shoulders and, getting into the car that the two men had just vacated, gave the driver brief instructions, and he drove off, disappearing round the corner.

'Don't like that bit of goods,' muttered the man with the scar. 'Too darn perky for me.'

'Don't waste time talking,' growled the chauffeur. 'I want to get off. Shall I go straight there?'

The thick-set man nodded as he got in after his companion. 'Yes, and put some pep into it,' he ordered crisply, closing the door after him with a bang.

The process of changing cars had occupied considerably less than fifteen seconds all told, and the side-turning chosen for the performance was so quiet and deserted that no one could have witnessed it. And even if someone had chanced to glance from one of the windows of the gloomy-looking houses on either side of the street, they would not have noticed anything particularly unusual. The whole operation had been carefully planned and carried out.

The saloon gathered speed rapidly, and while the driver slipped in and out of a maze of side-streets, keeping well away from the main thoroughfare, the two men in the back busied themselves securing Lowe with cords and a gag.

'The boss'll be pleased about this,' grunted the man with the scar. 'Got that bandage ready?'

The other held up a piece of thick folded material, which he secured tightly about the dramatist's eyes. 'There, he won't be able to see much through that,' he muttered. 'Better take those flowers with us when we get out.' He sniffed. 'Phew! I can smell that stuff now!'

They threw a piece of sacking over Lowe's body as additional protection against being seen, and then sat back and lighted cigarettes. 'Think he'll come round before we get there?' asked the man with the scar.

'No. He won't come out of that little snooze for a couple of hours yet, and if he does it don't matter. He's safe enough.'

By this time the car was far from the neighbourhood of Portland Place, and the driver, who seemed to be thoroughly familiar with the devious routes he picked out, put on extra speed. He drove right across London, and presently came to the squalid, dismal streets of Deptford.

When the car eventually turned into a deserted and dirty backyard, it was, oddly enough, little more than five minutes' walk from the warehouse at Cotton Street where Trevor Lowe had fallen into the hands of the gang for the first time. The yard where the saloon now pulled up was used as a refuse dump for piles of rubbish and old iron, and was flanked by a dilapidated building the tall chimney of which indicated that at one time the place had been a factory of some sort.

The still-unconscious dramatist was taken out of the car and carried through a narrow doorway and up a flight of stone steps leading to a lengthy passage with iron railings on one side that overlooked a deep pit strewn with bits of machinery, odd pipes and broken stone, the only remaining remnants of a once-extensive plant. At the end the passage turned sharp right, and continued past a flight of steps descending on the immediate left. Down these steps Lowe was taken till his bearers, panting with the exertion, rested their burden on the brick floor of a chamber, one wall of which was a mass of dark iron with one huge oblong door midway, which had a massive sliding grille.

Seizing the handles, the man with the scar pulled back the rusted metal bolts and slowly dragged the heavy door open, the joints of which emitted a clanking, grating sound. Breathing hard, he peered into the yawning blackness beyond and chuckled. 'He'll 'ave to be a bloomin' 'oudini to get out of that in a 'urry.' With the help of his companion, he shoved Lowe's limp body through the aperture and slammed and bolted the door.

'Now what do we do?' enquired the other, wiping his forehead.

'We've got to wait here till the boss comes,' said the man with the scar.

'What about the car outside? Won't that be seen? Be a bit awkward if a copper spotted it and came in here and found us.'

'That's all right,' retorted the other gruffly. 'The car's gone by now, and nobody's likely to come nosing about in here.' He glanced at his watch. 'What about a hand o' cards? We can use that stone bench over there for a table.' The other man nodded, and the scarred man produced a dirty pack of cards from his hip-pocket.

They played for nearly an hour, and then a noise on the steps leading down to the chamber caused them to stop and look up. A tall man in a black overcoat, his face hidden behind a handkerchief, stood in the doorway.

Al Brandt was feeling pleased. His plan had succeeded. The driver of the car had lost no time in telling him that everything had gone off without a hitch, and he, in his turn, had come post-haste to the disused factory. 'So we've got him, eh?' he said as he came forward. 'Is he in the furnace now?'

The man with the scar gave an evil grin and jerked his head. 'Yes, he's in there. The woman had got him under properly when we took over, and we tied him up and brought him straight here.'

Al Brandt's lips twisted into a smile behind his mask. He had been a bit dubious about employing Stella Feldman, but she had certainly played her part well. He went over to the iron door and pulled back the grille. The light from the small square windows at the end of the chamber was not enough to penetrate through the door of the furnace, and so Al Brandt flashed his pocket torch.

The circle of light focused on the dramatist's huddled form, and Brandt chuckled softly. 'Still unconscious, I suppose?' he muttered. 'Well, it's all the same, because we shan't be able to get him on board until after dark.' He paused, then went on, 'You and Farson will have to stop here all the time. At ten o'clock tonight I've arranged for him to be smuggled down to the river and onto the boat. She'll be underway at midnight for the West Indies.'

'You're not going to send him there, are you?' asked Farson in surprise. 'Plug him with a bullet. That's the safest thing.'

'When I want your advice I'll ask for it,' snapped Al Brandt. 'Trevor Lowe will not travel far, I can assure you of that. Now listen, Bryce. Just before you move him, give him the spray again. You've got it, I suppose?' Bryce nodded. 'Then I think that's all. Do nothing until you hear from me again, but don't leave this place unguarded. I'm taking no chances of him getting away this time.' He turned on his heel and, without another word, took his departure.

As the afternoon frayed into evening, Bryce and Farson began to feel hungry. 'Wish we'd thought to bring some grub with us,' grumbled Farson. 'Suppose you hang on here while I pop out and get a few sandwiches or something?'

Bryce turned on him furiously. ''Aven't you got any sense?' he snarled. 'Don't you know yer close to Cotton Street, which is swarming with cops? You go wandering about outside and the chances are you'll get nabbed. You're pretty well known to the police.'

'All right, keep yer 'air on!' growled Farson. 'I was only makin' a suggestion.

Blowed if I can see the idea of choosing this place, bang next door to Cotton Street, anyway.'

'If you want to know,' said Bryce, 'the boss chose this place because it's near the river. It's 'andy, that's the reason.' He glanced round at the iron grille suddenly as the slight sound of a movement came from the other side. 'He's coming out of it at last,' he remarked with a grin.

Trevor Lowe had, as a matter of fact, recovered from the powerful effects of the drug some minutes before, but had been too dazed to make any movement. Now he was struggling in the darkness in a vain attempt to free himself, but the gag had been tied so tightly round his mouth that he had difficulty in breathing, while the bandage across his eyes prevented him from seeing, even if there had been light enough within that dark and musty prison.

Sprawling there on the cold, hard iron rack of the disused furnace, he hadn't the faintest notion where he was or how long he had been there. In a little while, however, the searing, shooting pains in his head caused by the drug he had inhaled wore off slightly, and he remembered his recent experience with the woman in the car. How long ago had it all happened? It seemed like weeks, but Lowe knew it could have been only a matter of a few hours at the outside. Some latent sense of humour caused him even in this grim plight to smile inwardly at the thought of how easily he had been hoodwinked. It had certainly been a neat stroke on the part of the enemy.

The faint mumble of voices reached him and, straining his ears, he was able to catch the tail-end of the conversation between Bryce and Farson. So he was somewhere in the region of Cotton Street, was he? Well, that was something worth knowing at any rate, though how the information would help him was a question to which he found no immediate answer.

And what was that about the river? That didn't sound too hopeful. Already he had escaped from a watery grave by the skin of his teeth and the intervention of that other mystery woman, but there was little chance she would come again in the nick of time, and Al Brandt would no doubt be more thorough on this occasion.

Twisting on to his back, the dramatist wriggled till he felt his feet strike against something hard. Drawing up his knees slightly, he kicked, and the kick was followed by the dull, ringing sound of metal. Almost at once he heard footsteps and the grating sound of iron on iron. He could see nothing, but he heard a voice say roughly: 'If you don't keep still you'll get another dose!'

There was a clang, and Lowe heard the men retire a short distance away and converse in whispers. Frowning in the darkness, he tried to imagine where he was and what his prison was like. The iron rack underneath him, which was making his body stiff and sore, gave him a vague clue as to his whereabouts after a minute or so. That and the clang of the iron door, which couldn't be a solid door or he wouldn't be able to hear the voices after it was closed. It must be an iron grille of some description. So where could he be? Some kind of iron chamber evidently, but although he racked his brains he could not place it.

Again he tried to free himself, but after a few moments gave it up, breathless and exhausted. The cords had been expertly tied and not a single strand weakened.

On and off for the next hour Lowe continued the struggle, and the perspiration was streaming down his forehead when he paused to listen to fresh voices that suddenly came faintly from outside. He stopped, breathing hard and straining his ears. He heard the sound of scuffling footsteps, shouting and muffled curses. A pistol shot rang out and a bullet thudded with a sharp tang against the iron grille, and then quite suddenly the sound of conflict ceased, except for the excited voices.

Trevor Lowe heard someone approach his prison, unclamp the bolts, and throw open the heavy door. For a second there was silence, and then the familiar voice of White shouted: 'All right, Mr. Lowe, we'll soon get you out!'

24

The Phone Message

Trevor Lowe felt hands grope forward and seize him by the ankles. He was dragged, then lifted bodily through the doorway of his prison and placed upright on his feet, in which position he was held while his cords were cut through and the bandages removed from his mouth and eyes. After a vigorous massage, his muscles lost some of their stiffness, and he was able to move in comfort.

'White, I don't know what brought you here,' he said, looking about him, 'but I've never been more pleased to see you in my life. Four policemen, too,' he added, 'and if I'm not mistaken, my shy friend, Mr. Jelf!' He smiled as he saw the scowling and handcuffed forms of Bryce and Farson at the far end of the chamber between two burly constables. 'And my two gaolers all nicely secured. Quite a good bit of work.'

He had a little talk with the policemen, and a few seconds later Bryce and Farson were marched off to the station, leaving Lowe, White and the man Jelf alone. The latter was still looking a little scared, but at the same time rather proud of himself.

'So this was the place they put me in, eh?' remarked the dramatist, looking through the door of the furnace. 'Hm, I wondered what it was!'

He wandered out of the stoking chamber where he had been standing, and up the stone steps on the right to the gallery, where he spent some seconds surveying the dilapidated remains of broken brick and rusted machinery in the pit below. Presently, turning on his heel, he went back and joined White and Jelf. 'I think we'll get out of this place and go back to Portland Place now,' he said. 'And, Jelf, you had better come along as well. You can make yourself useful if you don't decide to run away again.'

Outside at the end of the street they found a taxi waiting. 'I thought it would be better than having it outside, where it would attract attention,' said White; and Lowe nodded agreement.

As the cab picked its way through the dingy streets the dramatist sat back and regarded the other two thoughtfully. 'Now, White,' he said, 'I'm waiting to hear how you managed to find me, and how Mr. Jelf happens to be a member of the expedition. Let me hear all about it.'

White grinned, and the nervous Jelf showed considerable signs of agitation, blushing a deep and beautiful crimson. 'As a matter of fact, I only played a secondary part,' said the secretary modestly. 'It was Jelf who really did all the work. Perhaps he'd better explain what happened himself.'

Jelf coughed uneasily. 'All right, sir, I'll tell you,' he began nervously. 'When you went to get your 'at and coat, I somehow got all flurried like. I didn't want to go to Scotland Yard, with all them detectives an' things, an' so I bunked off while the going was good, if you follow me.'

'I'm ahead of you,' said Lowe. 'Go on.'

'Well, sir,' continued Jelf, 'when I got down the street I began to think better of it an' decided to come back. I was a few yards away from your place when I sees a car, with a woman an' two men. They was talking, like, but it was the thick-set man with the scar that caught my eye and set me a-thinkin'; and then I remembered having seen 'im before, hanging about several times outside Mr. Marlow's place.'

'That was before Mr. Marlow was killed, I take it?' asked Lowe, and the man nodded his head emphatically.

'Yes, it was before that,' he said, "cause at the time I didn't take much notice. But when I read what had 'appened to Mr. Marlow, it struck me — like a blow on the 'ead, it did — that this fellow with the scarred face had been watchin', if you follow me.'

'I see,' murmured the dramatist.

'Well, I recognised 'im at once,' went on Jelf, 'and I wondered what he was doin' there. I 'opped down a side turning and kept my eye on that little party. It was just then that I saw you, sir, from the end of the turning, start walking down Portland Place. I was wondering what I'd better do, when I saw the man with the scar catch hold of the woman by the arm an' point quickly after you.'

'I think I know what happened after that,' said Lowe with a smile. 'She got into the car and came along after me while her two companions got into another car and followed at a distance.'

'That's right, sir,' said Jelf. 'And when I saw the car with the woman stop, and saw her speak to you, and you get inside and shut the door and drive off with that other car following behind, I thought to myself, something's wrong about this.'

'You were right there,' said the dramatist. 'What did you do then?'

'Got into a taxi an' followed too,' said Jelf promptly.

'Ah, now I begin to understand!' broke in Lowe. 'You acted very sensibly, Jelf. But don't let me interrupt you.'

Jelf, who had gained considerable courage while talking, finished his story with dramatic gestures of his hands. 'I followed in the cab, though I nearly got in a fix at one stage. Down a side street, just as the taxi I was in was rounding the corner, I saw the two motorcars I was following draw up alongside one another and the men and woman change over. They was a long way down the street, an' there was nobody about, but they was right smart about that changeover. When the cars got going again, the woman went off to the right, while the other car went straight on. For a moment I was properly puzzled to know which to go after, then I realised all in a flash, as you might say, that you hadn't got out, and so I decided yours was the one to keep my eye on.'

Mr. Jelf paused for breath and concluded: 'And that's pretty well all there is to it, sir. I saw the car turn into the yard of that disused factory, and I knew there was dirty work going on somehow, if you follow me. So I raced back as quick as I could and told this gentleman all about it.'

As he finished, he jerked a thumb at White, and Lowe smiled with approval.

'You've done splendidly,' he said, 'and you will certainly have to be compensated for all your time, trouble, and — er — expense. But we'll go into all that later on. In the meantime, I want you to promise not to run away again — not that I think you're contemplating it for one moment — because you're going to be useful sometime tonight.'

As soon as they reached Portland Place, Lowe got on the phone to Shadgold. Hurriedly he related the details of his latest adventure, and the Yard man gasped with astonishment at the other end of the wire.

'Al Brandt seems to be making a dead set at you,' he said. 'You'll have to be careful. I wonder who the woman was?'

'Just someone hired for the occasion, I should imagine,' replied Lowe.

'Suppose so,' grunted Shadgold. 'Anyhow, I'll get on to those two fellows that were collared and question them right away.'

'There won't be any need,' said the dramatist. 'It'll only be a waste of time, and anyway, you won't get a grain of anything useful out of them; they know no more about Brandt than Schwartz and the other man.'

'Don't follow you,' said Shadgold gruffly. 'What do you mean, there won't be any need?'

Lowe smiled grimly into the mouthpiece.

'Merely that we're going to put our hands on Al Brandt tonight,' he said calmly.

There came a snort of surprise from his listener. 'How?' he demanded.

'The idea of keeping me a prisoner in that furnace was so that I could be smuggled down to the river after dark,' explained Lowe. 'Now what I suggest you do, Shadgold, is to get half a dozen men and come with me down to Deptford. We'll post ourselves round the factory, and when Brandt comes along to supervise the final rites for my decease we'll get him. It'll be easy, because he naturally won't be aware of the fact that I've been released.'

'I see,' said Shadgold quickly. 'But supposing he doesn't come himself?'

'He'll come,' said Lowe with conviction. 'He won't risk failure at this stage by leaving the final arrangements to others.'

'You're probably right,' agreed the Yard man. 'What time do you think we should start?'

'Now,' said Trevor Lowe. 'I'll pick you up at the Yard.' He hung up the receiver, and turning to White, briefly explained what he proposed to do.

'And while I'm gone,' he ended, 'I want you to remain here and keep Jelf company. I shall probably be back some time before eleven o'clock.'

★ ★ ★

About three quarters of an hour after Lowe had departed from the factory yard at Deptford with White and Jelf, a man made his way leisurely along the crowded main street. He turned to the left by a public house on the corner and continued in the direction of Cotton Street, but long before he reached that rank and unsalubrious thoroughfare he turned down another side street, finally emerging into the narrow, deserted back lane which ran past what had once been Finney & Webster's smelting works.

Glancing casually over his shoulder to see if he was noticed, he slipped through the entrance into the yard. After some minutes he came out again, but as he hurried away he no longer moved with a leisurely, casual gait. He walked swiftly, keeping close to the wall and peering every now and then through the dim shadows of the descending night as if he was uncertain what they might hold. So rapidly did he depart, that he was clear of the immediate vicinity within a tenth of the time he had taken to come; and when he had gone, the dilapidated factory and yard once more became silent and forsaken, inhabited only by the dim and loose shadows of the misty night.

But it did not remain so for any great length of time. Later there came another figure that stole quietly into the yard and vanished, and a few seconds later yet another that slipped unseen to follow in the wake of the first. And so they came, one after the other, stealthily and from all directions, and passed into the vast, rambling building beyond. Six of them entered thus, and then two men came together, with coat-collars well up and hats down over their eyes. A nearby clock chimed the hour of eight, and when the last note died away the place lapsed into stillness that was only broken by a distant clatter of traffic and the faint sound of a brawl that was taking place outside a public house in the region of Cotton Street, three turnings off.

Nine o'clock came and went ... ten o'clock ... half-past; and at eleven in the candle-lighted stoking chamber, Inspector Shadgold rose stiffly. 'Afraid something must have gone wrong, Mr. Lowe,' he growled. 'They're not coming.'

The dramatist, who had been walking moodily up and down for the last hour, frowned and bit his lip. 'I believe you're right,' he muttered. 'Brandt must have been warned that his plans had gone wrong. It's no use staying now.' Shadgold grunted disgustedly.

And then, suddenly, there came the sound of approaching steps, rapid stumbling steps as though the owner was in a great hurry. Instantly alert, Lowe and Shadgold swung round towards the entrance. The man who presently crossed the threshold was not the man they were expecting. It was one of the plain-clothes detectives, and with him came White.

'Hello,' said Lowe in surprise. 'What are you doing here?'

'Preventing you wasting your time,' said the secretary. 'Brandt isn't coming back here.'

'How do you know?' snapped Shadgold.

'Got a phone message about an hour and a half ago,' explained White. 'A woman rang up and said she wanted to speak to you, Mr. Lowe. I said you were out. At first she wouldn't say anything more, but when I told her I was your secretary she changed her mind and gave me a message. She said would I tell you that Al Brandt would be at Bell's Wharf, Vauxhall, sometime after midnight. She said you were not to get there before twelve, and that it would be as well if you didn't go alone.'

'Did she say anything else?' asked Lowe quickly.

White shook his head. 'No, that's all,' he replied. 'I had a lot to say, but she rang off.'

The dramatist turned excitedly to Shadgold. 'That message came from the woman who saved my life in Cotton Street,' he said. 'Come on! Get your men together and we'll make for Bell's Wharf at once.'

The Scotland Yard man looked dubious. 'It may only be a ruse to get us away from here,' he suggested.

'I don't think so,' said Lowe. 'That woman, whoever she is, knows more about Al Brandt than any of us. If she says that he'll be at Bell's Wharf shortly after midnight, you can bet your life he will.' He crossed over to the door. 'If we leave at once,' he went on, 'we ought to get to Vauxhall at about half-past twelve. Personally, I don't think this message is a fake. With a bit of luck, tonight ought to see the end of Mr. Al Brandt for good!'

A few minutes later, leaving White, despite his protests, to return to Portland Place and keep an eye on Jelf, Lowe, Shadgold and more of the plain-clothes men set off in the police car for Bell's Wharf.

25

Brandt Decides to Quit

Mr. Felix Anstruther splashed a lavish portion of whisky into the glass that stood before him, set down the decanter with a hand that was none too steady, and swallowed the neat spirit in one gulp. With narrowed eyes that saw nothing of the comfort of the room in which he sat, he stared across the flat-topped writing-table, chewing mechanically at his well-manicured thumb-nail.

Mr. Anstruther was a tall man with a thin, sallow face, the lower part of which was concealed beneath a neatly trimmed beard and moustache. No one who had known him two years ago would have recognised in this grey-haired, soldierly-looking man the notorious Al Brandt who had left the speakeasy on Chicago's waterfront, the rain falling about his ears and the words of a woman's threat filling his soul with terror.

And yet it *was* the same man, and many times since the night on which Mike Ahearn had been sent to his death had the picture of the white-faced woman who had been the man's wife risen like a ghost before Al Brandt's eyes.

He had left Chicago on the following day — left it because he was in fear of his life. His own gang had gone over in a body to his rival, and they were out after him. The news reached him early in the morning brought by the one man who had remained faithful to his chief, a dope-sodden little hunchback. So when the sun rose, Brandt's powerful car had carried him many miles away from the city that had become for him a place of doom.

Harry, the little hunchback who had warned him, had pleaded in vain to be allowed to accompany him, but Brandt wanted no encumbrances. Three days later in New York, he had read in a newspaper an account of the man's death. He had been riddled with bullets from a passing car as he was walking down Main Street; and although he knew that Harry had died because he had been faithful, Brandt read the account without flinching.

It was in New York that he received his first warning that Kit Ahearn had not forgotten. He found it pinned to the door of the cheap attic in which he was hiding, and it sent him flying from New York in a panic. He went to Madrid, where six months later he almost came face to face with her as he was entering his hotel. Spain saw him no more, and from country to country he fled, pursued by the woman whose husband he had killed.

Eventually he arrived in England, broken and penniless, his dark hair grey with the strain of the life he had been leading. By slow degrees he put into practice the scheme that had matured in his brain during the lonely hours when he had been forced to walk the streets of London, not having the money to pay for a bed. And then, when everything had been going better than he had hoped, when money was rolling in practically for the asking, when he was beginning to hope that he had at last eluded the woman whose vengeance he feared more than anything on earth, had come that warning: 'Remember Mike Ahearn.'

He shivered as he stared at the writing-table before him. *Remember Mike Ahearn.*

Remember him? Great heavens, if only he could forget him! If only that grisly ghost that haunted his waking hours and denied him the comforting oblivion of sleep could be laid to rest!

He poured out more whisky and raised the glass to his lips. Then reluctantly he set it down. He must take no more of the stuff, although the temptation was great. He must keep his head clear. The time had arrived for action. London was getting too hot. He must quit while there was yet time.

A few days ago had brought the news that Schwartz and Slater had been arrested. Well, they knew nothing that could put the police on his track. He had been very careful to keep his identity a secret. Only Marlow had known — confound him! — and anyway, he was dead now. As for the others, to them he was known only as 'the boss'.

It was a nuisance that the warehouse at Cotton Street had fallen into the hands of the police. The secret store of cocaine had, of course, been confiscated, and that meant the loss of thousands of pounds. Trevor Lowe, too, had managed to escape on that occasion from the cellar. How he had managed it was a mystery. He must have had outside help. Damned interfering amateur!

Brandt frowned and set down the glass that he had been holding half-raised to his lips, having mechanically picked it up again while he was thinking. He certainly must leave that stuff alone. Too much of that spelled disaster. What did it matter how Lowe had got away? The question now was, did the police know anything about the other place at Vauxhall? Had anyone split? If they did, it was serious. If not, then things were fairly plain sailing.

There was a lot of money at the Vauxhall place — with the exception of a few hundreds which Brandt kept by in the wall-safe; all the money he had. True, only part of it belonged to him — one third to be exact. The other two thirds should be distributed among the rest of the gang, but he would possibly find a chance of getting away with the lot. The money was concealed in the inner room in a place that he alone knew about. But had Schwartz and Slater kept their mouths shut?

He rose from his chair and began to walk up and down, pausing presently to glance at his watch. Half-past eight. There was plenty of time yet. He went over to the picture that concealed the wall-safe, moved it aside, and, taking a key from his pocket, inserted it in the tiny hole and pulled open the heavy circular steel door. There was nothing in the safe except a roll of notes kept in place by a rubber band. Al Brandt did not believe in keeping a collection of papers. That was evidence that was better destroyed. He took the notes, put them in his pocket, and pushed the safe shut.

Going out into the hall, he pulled on a heavy coat, for it was raining, and, switching out the lights, he left the flat and was carried down to the street in an automatic lift. The damp made his wounded hand ache as he hurried along Piccadilly towards the entrance of a lighted restaurant, and he cursed Gregory's bullet that had passed through the fleshy part of his hand.

He ate a good dinner, but drank sparingly from the bottle of light wine he had ordered. He took his time, and it was nearly eleven when he left the restaurant and turned his steps towards Westminster. And with him, its hand outstretched to grasp him, went the shadow of death.

★　★　★

Gregory Carr felt fed up; had felt fed up all day. There was no real reason why he should, because that particular morning had brought him a stroke of luck that two days before would have set him walking on air. A letter had arrived from a firm of advertising contractors to whom he had written over a month previously for a job, and from whom he never expected to hear again, offering him the situation at a salary he had never dreamed of.

It had dispersed all his worries. He would be able to remain in his pleasant little flat, and see all his creditors and arrange to pay off his debts. Yet in spite of this rosy change in his future, he felt as depressed as if he were due for execution the following day.

It was at lunchtime that he finally ran the cause of this depression to earth. It was something of a shock when he realised that the whole cause of it was the woman in the red hat! He wanted to see her again, though the possibility that he ever would seemed very remote.

He came back from his lunch and prowled restlessly about his flat, trying to devise ways by which he could get in touch with her. He thought of every conceivable plan, but the only one that seemed to offer any chance at all was an advertisement in the papers. With a pencil he drafted one out: 'Will the woman in the red hat communicate with G.C.' He tried half a dozen times on similar lines, altering the wording each time, then stopped and tore the whole lot up. Perhaps she didn't want to see him again, and in that case it would be no good advertising. Besides, she might think it was a trap, and that he had done it at the instigation of the police.

This sent his thoughts in another direction. What was the reason for her avoidance of the law? What was the secret she held that made her so anxious that the police should not be called in to deal with that gang of cut-throats? Apparently she had nothing whatever to do with them, for neither of the men who had come to his flat had recognised her. What, then, was her connection with them?

Gregory found no satisfactory answer to any of these questions, and at eight o'clock got so sick of his own company and his own thoughts that he jammed on his hat and went out. He had no particular object in view, but after walking for some time found himself at Oxford Circus and decided that he would drop in and see Trevor Lowe. Here he was unlucky, however.

Reaching the house in Portland Place, he rang the bell, and presently the housekeeper came to the door. In answer to his query, she informed him that both Lowe and White were out, and she didn't know when they would be back.

Gregory continued his aimless walk. He strolled up to Marble Arch, and went through the Park, taking a circuitous route and eventually coming out at Hyde Park

Corner. It was getting on for half-past ten by now, and he had decided that there was nothing else to do but return to his flat and fill in the next hour with a book. But then one of those coincidences that are so common in real life, and surprise no one except book reviewers, occurred: he saw the woman in the red hat!

She was in the act of stepping into a taxi, and the light from a street standard shone full on her face as she turned to give the driver his directions. There was no mistake — it was the woman who had occupied Gregory's thoughts most of that day.

Acting on a sudden impulse, he hailed a cab that was crawling slowly towards him. 'You see that taxi just drawing away from the kerb — over there by the station?' he said rapidly to the driver, and the man nodded. 'Well, follow it,' snapped Gregory, and sprang inside.

The cab swung round and, as the other turned and went swiftly in the direction of Victoria, ran smoothly along in its wake. And so, quite accidentally, Gregory started on the adventure of his life.

26

Gregory Finds More Trouble

The tail-light of the taxi containing the woman in the red hat was clearly visible to Gregory as he leaned forward in his own cab, and he wondered where this impulsive chase would end. Not in his wildest imaginings did he guess the truth, or have the faintest inkling of what the night held in store.

They were nearing Vauxhall Station when the cab in front slowed and, drawing into the kerb, came to a halt almost opposite the station entrance. Gregory tapped hurriedly on the window and his own cab also stopped. The woman he was following had already got out, and as Gregory paid his driver, he saw her cross the street and walk quickly along the road that led to Battersea. He set off in her wake.

Exactly what he was going to do, he had not decided. All he knew was that lucky chance had allowed him to find the woman again, and he wasn't going to lose sight of her until he had discovered where she lived. Another opportunity such as this might never present itself.

As he strode along a hundred yards behind her, he took stock of the surrounding neighbourhood with growing astonishment. This was no residential quarter, not even the meanest. There was nothing here but big factories and warehouses. What in the world, then, was the woman doing here, and where was she going? Why hadn't she let the taxi carry her to her destination, wherever it was, instead of dismissing it at Vauxhall Station and continuing on foot?

There was no hesitation about her movements. She was walking hurriedly, determinedly, as though her destination was clearly fixed in her mind. Hugging the high brick wall, broken here and there by the gates leading to yards and wharfs, went Gregory on her trail — and then suddenly she vanished!

A clanking tramcar had just gone past and he had turned for a second to look at it. Before he turned, the woman was there. When he looked again, she was gone, and the road ahead empty!

Gregory muttered something unprintable below his breath and increased his pace, pausing at the spot where he had last seen her. A narrow alleyway led into the blackness, and after a second's hesitation he turned into it.

This must have been the way she had gone. There was no other opening or turning. It was very dark and sloped downwards. He smelt the tang of the river, and heard the *flop-flop* of water against wooden piles and the creak of a moored barge as it rose and fell on the tide. Ahead, several lights twinkled, and then he came out onto a rotting wharf. But there was no sign of the woman he had followed.

Gregory stood on the brink of the wharf and looked about, feeling thoroughly annoyed. He had lost her, there was no doubt about that. Where the deuce she had gone, he hadn't the faintest idea. To his left rose the high wall of a warehouse, and to his right the wharf continued irregularly into the darkness. That was apparently the only direction she could have taken.

He picked his way carefully among the strewn debris that littered the landing stage, pausing every now and again to listen.

No sound but the lap of the river came to his ears, and presently he found his further progress barred by a jutting fence. He retraced his steps, cursing himself for having lost this opportunity. Where had the woman gone? It was an extraordinary place for her to have come at that hour — more extraordinary than the fact that, having entered the dim alley, she should have apparently vanished from the face of the earth.

He made his way back to the street, feeling carefully along the sides of the narrow lane in case he had missed some turning or door through which the woman could have gone. He found a door about halfway along, but if she had gone that way she must have locked it after her, for it was firm under his pressure. With a grunt of disgust he gave it up and, coming back into the main street, began to walk towards Vauxhall. What on earth the woman was doing wandering about among those deserted factories and storehouses, shut for the night and given over to rats and darkness, he couldn't imagine.

He had gone about two hundred yards when his attention was attracted by two men in the act of crossing over the road. He gave them but a casual glance until they came under the light of one of the few street standards, and then something familiar about them touched a chord in his memory. He looked more closely, and with a sudden start realised that they were the two gangsters whom he had laid out in his flat.

They were a good way away, but coming towards him. With his pulse beating an irregular rhythm of excitement, Gregory hurriedly crossed over to the shadow of the opposite side of the road. From the cover of a doorway, he watched them draw level with him; then, as they passed and went on, he turned and followed them.

He had made no mistake: they were the two. What were they doing in this neighbourhood? Was there any connection between their presence and the presence of the woman? Gregory couldn't pass it off as a coincidence. There *was* a connection, and he made up his mind to find out more. There was something in the air tonight, and fate had given him the chance to get mixed up in it. He would take the chance that had been offered.

Warily, he followed the two shuffling figures. He hadn't far to go, for near the alley down which the woman had gone they paused and also turned into the narrow opening. Gregory waited for nearly five minutes after they had disappeared before he approached the place cautiously and once again entered that dark aperture. As he had expected, the two gangsters had vanished.

He crept towards the door and tested it. It was fast as before, but he felt certain — just as certain as if he had been present — that it had been opened and shut again, and that that was the way through which the men had gone. And the way the woman in the red hat had gone, too.

That was a disturbing thought. Somewhere on the other side of that door was the woman, as well as — either known or unknown to her — two men who Gregory had had proof were not in the least well disposed towards her. And the door was locked. He couldn't get in to render her assistance even if she should need it.

Gregory frowned. There was only one way to find out what lay beyond that door, and that was to seek some other means of entrance. Perhaps there was a way from the street. He retraced his steps and walked on a few yards past the mouth of the alley. A little further along, he came upon a pair of heavy padlocked gates bearing the words 'Bell's Wharf' in dingy white lettering.

He glanced quickly about and saw that there was no one in sight. The next second he had pulled himself astride the gates and dropped into the yard beyond. A huge building faced him, dark and gloomy, and it was obvious that the door in the alley gave entrance to the place. He moved forward across the yard, carefully avoiding the heaps of straw and broken boxes with which it was littered. He was determined, if possible, to get inside that building and find out what was taking place.

There was not a sound anywhere, but he knew that there were at least three people somewhere on the premises. It was very dark here, and he could scarcely see

284

anything, but he felt his way along the wall that reared its bulk into the night. He had negotiated two sides when the brickwork suddenly vanished, and his arm went into empty space. Gregory paused and found himself outside a window, the glass of which had long since gone. With infinite caution, he climbed through, and stepped into a void of blackness that was like velvet. He took two steps forward, and then stopped dead as the muffled sound of a woman's scream reached his ears. It was a sharp cry of fear and terror, and it ended abruptly as though a hand had been hastily clapped over her mouth to smother the noise.

Gregory felt his skin go cold. Something horrible was happening nearby. The woman in the red hat was in deadly peril, to judge by that cry.

He took a few stumbling steps into the blackness — and then the floor beneath his feet gave way! A blaze of light engulfed him as he fell, and he heard a startled shout. Then his head struck something hard, and like the snuffing of a candle, all went black!

27

The Fight in the Cellar

Gregory was only momentarily stunned. The blackness dissolved into grey and then into a blaze of light, and he found himself sprawling at the foot of a flight of steps in a low-ceilinged brick cellar.

'Good evening, Mr. Carr,' said a rasping voice. 'You seem destined to turn up at the most inopportune moments.'

Gregory blinked in the direction of the voice and saw the tall form of the masked gang leader standing by an overturned packing-case. The cellar was half-full of rough-looking men, and over in one corner, held firmly between the two gangsters he had followed to the place, was the woman in the red hat.

Gregory scrambled dazedly to his feet. 'What are you doing with that woman?' he demanded tersely.

'Teaching her to mind her own

business,' retorted Al Brandt. 'It's a lesson that you would also find it useful to learn.'

The sneering tone sent a wave of rage through Gregory, and he took a step forward with clenched fists. But strong fingers gripped his arms from behind and he was jerked back.

'Since you have arrived at an opportune moment,' went on the sneering voice, 'you will be able to learn the lesson together.'

'You brute!' The cry came in a strangled voice from the white-faced woman. 'You cowardly brute! Where is my brother? What have you done with him?'

Brandt swung round and deliberately struck her across the mouth. 'Your brother was killed — down in Deptford,' he snarled. 'I served him the same way as I'm going to serve you. He was a poor, weak-kneed fool, sodden with drugs, and would have been a traitor as well if a knife hadn't stopped him!'

The woman's face, white before, went deathly pale except for the livid mark of the blow, but her eyes blazed. 'Killed!' Her lips scarcely more than formed the word. 'You mean Jim is — dead!'

'I do,' snapped Al Brandt, 'and it's the best thing that could have happened to him. He was a whining cur — frightened at his own shadow.' He laughed harshly. 'You'll be able to tell him what I say when you meet him. Shall I show you what I'm going to do with you? Look!'

He took a step forward, and, stooping, pulled at an iron ring in the floor. A trap-door came up slowly, and with it a cold waft of air — heavy and fetid with the smell of river mud and stagnant slime. The rushing, gurgling sound of water reached Gregory's ears.

'That's where you are going, my pretty lady,' said Al Brandt. 'Down into the mud. And since he's here, your interfering friend can join you!'

The woman gave a gasping cry and swayed between the two men who held her. Gregory saw red. 'You devil!' he burst out, struggling frantically to free himself. 'If I could only get my hands on you — '

'You can't,' said the gang leader, 'and this time I'm going to make certain that you never will.'

He rapped out an order, and Gregory was flung violently to the floor. Mad with rage, he lashed out with his foot, and one of the men who had approached him reeled back, cursing horribly, holding his shattered jaw. But against those odds he was powerless to do much. A dozen hands seized him and held him down, and despite his struggles, his ankles and wrists were bound securely.

'Weight him,' snarled Al Brandt, 'and weight him well. The mud is deep — let him sink far into it.' There was a pile of rusty scrap iron in one corner, and the gangsters stuffed Gregory's pockets with the larger pieces. 'Now do the same with the woman,' said Brandt. 'They may as well go together.'

They found her an easier job than Gregory, for she had fainted under the shock and was lying on the floor in a limp heap.

Gregory watched the diabolical preparations. A shuddering fear had come over him — not for himself, but for the woman. It was the end. Life was over, with all its hopes and joys, efforts and high ambitions. And now, just at the end, when it was too late, something else had come into his life — something that might have heightened all the joys and softened all the sorrows . . .

'You devil!' he gasped, his voice half choked with hot rebellion against this awful thing that surged up within him. 'Let that woman alone, you — '

A filthy rag was forced into his mouth and tied there, strangling the rest of his words. 'I'm sorry that I can't listen to what you have to say, Mr. Carr,' mocked Brandt, 'but time is short. I have a lot to do in a very little while — you have all eternity.' He turned to the men who had been binding the woman. 'Have you finished? Good! Bring them both over to the trap.'

Gregory was seized and dragged roughly over the floor until his head was overhanging the black void and the noise of rushing water swelled to a roar in his ears. A movement near at hand made him twist his head. The woman in the red hat had been laid beside him. She appeared to be still unconscious, for her eyes were closed, and Gregory prayed that she might remain so until unconsciousness drifted into everlasting oblivion.

Al Brandt bent over him, and Gregory saw the cruel glint of the eyes behind the mask. 'This is where you make a quick exit, my friend,' he hissed. 'Perhaps your death will be a warning to others, for as sure as they interfere with my business they will die.'

'I hope that will not apply to me,' said a clear, incisive voice, 'because I'm going to do a lot of interfering, and I don't want to die yet!'

Brandt swung round with an oath. The face of Trevor Lowe was looking down at him through the open trap in the ceiling, and a long-barrelled pistol was pointing steadily at his head.

'Put up your hands, Brandt,' snapped the dramatist sharply, 'and do it quickly! The whole place is surrounded. If I raise my voice, the men will think there's something wrong, and they might get rough.'

Al Brandt slowly raised his arms. 'All right,' he began, 'I'll — ' And then with a lightning movement he shot out his right leg and kicked over the packing-case on which the lamp was standing.

There was a crash of breaking glass, a thin flicker of blue flame, and then pitch darkness. Trevor Lowe fired at random, and the sound of the shots brought a rush of feet as the men he had brought with him hurried to see what was the matter.

'Come on, Shadgold!' cried the dramatist. 'The whole bunch are down below.' He began to stumble down the steps into the confused babel of sound that drifted up through the open trap. A bullet whistled by his head, and he fired in the direction of the flash. There was a scream of pain, followed by a fusillade of lead that hummed and smacked on all sides. A bullet snicked his right ear, and he felt the warm blood as it trickled down between his collar and his neck. It was a miracle that his injury wasn't more severe, but the next moment he was in the middle of a seething, cursing crowd of fighting humanity.

The gangsters had stopped shooting, for now they couldn't tell who was friend and who was foe. Then one of the detectives threw some light on the scene from an electric torch. After that it was only a matter of moments. The Scotland Yard men outnumbered the gangsters by nearly two to one.

'Quite a nice little bag,' panted Inspector Shadgold as he gazed at the handcuffed, sullen-faced men grouped against one wall. 'But what's happened to the big boss of the outfit? He's the fellow I want.'

'There's a door over there,' said Trevor Lowe, dabbing at his wounded ear with a handkerchief. 'He's probably gone through there.'

'Break it down,' ordered Shadgold when he found it was locked.

It took them some time, for it was solidly built, and then they found another cellar beyond, a little smaller than the first. In this, too, was a door, but it was open, and a cold breeze with the tang of the river in it blew in. There was no sign of the gang leader. Nor did they find him on the wharf. Al Brandt had disappeared.

28

The Getaway

As the light went out, Al Brandt dropped to his knees and made his way, in a crouching position, to the door at the far end of the cellar. Regardless of the rising hubbub that was going on behind him, he took a key from his pocket, and by his sense of touch found the lock. A second later he had slipped through the door and relocked it behind him.

He cared not a jot for the men whom he had left to their fate in the other cellar. They would fall into the hands of the police; and, so far as he was concerned, that was the best thing that could happen to them. He had meant to make his getaway tonight anyhow, and, but for the fact that he had found the woman spying round the place in search of her brother, he would have been gone long since. He hadn't known that Cornish had had a sister, but her knowledge of the warehouse showed that she must have been there before. Probably followed her brother to try and save him from himself. Oh well, to hell with her and all the rest of them! With a little luck he could get clear away, and the delay caused by the woman would prove profitable after all.

He smiled as he went over to a corner of the cellar and felt about for a rusty nail that projected from the brickwork. A sharp pull and a brick came out in his hand. Beyond was a deep cavity stuffed full of notes of large denominations. Here were the proceeds of the gang's many operations, less a certain amount that had been disbursed for working expenses, and a good part of it should have been shared out with the others. Brandt had thought long about how he could double-cross his associates and get away with the lot, and now the arrival of the police had solved the problem for him.

His motorboat was waiting at the wharf, and with the money in his pocket he could run down river to Gravesend and pick up some boat that would take him out of the country. Kit Ahearn would never find him then. He would elude them all and spend the rest of his life in the comfort that was his to buy.

The sound of muffled shots from behind the door made him hurry. He pulled the money out feverishly and stuffed it into his pocket. Going over to the exit that led onto the wharf, he shot back the bolt and twisted the catch.

A drizzle of rain was falling, and the night was so dark that he couldn't see more than a few feet before him. He pushed the door shut behind him, failing to notice that the spring lock hadn't caught because the bolt had slipped forward. Crossing the rickety landing-stage, he paused at the head of the ladder. The *lap-lap* of the river came up to him, and he could just make out the shape of the powerful boat swinging below.

Tearing off the silken mask from his face, he flung it away and began to descend the ladder. The little craft swayed as he stepped into it. Hurriedly, he undid the painter and started the tiny engine. Seating himself behind the wheel, he sent the little boat *chug-chugging* into midstream.

The rain had increased in violence and was coming down in torrents, and for this Al Brandt was grateful. Steering well in under the shadow of the barges that lined the riverbank, he headed downstream, keeping a sharp lookout for any signs of pursuit. He saw a tugboat with a string of barges behind it coming towards him, and the wash as it passed sent his little craft bobbing up and down like a cork and almost capsized it. He managed to right it, however, and went on, increasing his speed slightly.

It was important that he should reach Gravesend before dawn. Once the light was in the sky, he would be seen by passing craft and more easily traced if the police made any enquiries. The money in his pockets gave him confidence. It shouldn't be a difficult matter to get out of the country, and once he was away there would be very little fear of his being found.

On through the splashing rain ran the boat, and just as the sky was lightening in the east he came to the outskirts of Gravesend. Slowing his engine until the little propeller was only just revolving, he searched about in the pale light for a place where he could land unobserved. And presently he found it, a stretch of deserted riverbank. He twisted the helm and ran the boat towards the shore until its nose bumped gently into the bank.

Stopping the engine, he got out, and, stooping, pulling out the plug. As the water began to wash the bottom of the little launch, he restarted the engine, gave a twist to the wheel, and watched it as it went slowly out towards midstream. It was filling rapidly, and a little beyond the middle of the river suddenly disappeared below the surface, leaving nothing to mark the spot except the swirling of the water above the place where it had gone down.

Al Brandt nodded his satisfaction and began to make his way towards the town. He was cold and hungry, shivering with the clamminess of his rain-soaked clothing. The first thing he needed was a meal and warmth. After that he would have to try and get a little sleep; his eyes were hot and as heavy as lead.

He came into Gravesend just as the early workers were beginning to set out on their day's occupation, and in a turning off the main street he found the type of place he was looking for — a small hotel used mostly by seamen. He engaged a room and ordered breakfast. When he had eaten it and swallowed two cups of steaming coffee, he felt better.

The time was only a little after five, and he decided that he could get three hours' sleep before the shops would be open and he could think about purchasing some new clothes and the various things he would need for his getaway. Leaving instructions that he was to be called at eight, he locked himself in his bare little bedroom, and three minutes later was in bed and sleeping the sleep of utter exhaustion.

While he slept dreamlessly and undisturbed, there came into Gravesend a small car, mud-spattered and dirty. And the figure at the wheel, did he but know it, represented for Al Brandt the figure of the Angel of Death!

29

Pursuit!

A tired and dispirited party gathered in Detective-Inspector Shadgold's bare and cheerless office at Scotland Yard. The burly inspector, his eyes heavy and weary, sat at his desk twisting a pen-holder between his stubby fingers and looking across at Trevor Lowe, who was seated in the only other chair the room boasted.

Gregory Carr, very little the worse for his ordeal, had offered to see the woman home; and since there was nothing more that could be learned from him, or any other way in which he could help, Shadgold had agreed. 'Well, we've got the smaller fry, but the big fish has slipped through our fingers,' he growled despondently. 'He must have gone by way of the river.'

'I think that's pretty certain,' agreed Lowe, nodding. 'Have you notified the Thames Police to keep a lookout?'

Shadgold inclined his bullet head. 'Phoned 'em from a call-box immediately after the raid,' he said briefly. 'They'll report here at once if they find any trace.'

'There's one other chance,' began the dramatist, and stopped.

The inspector's drooping eyelids widened with a jerk, and he shot a quick glance at his friend. 'What do you mean?' he grunted.

'The woman,' said Lowe slowly. 'The woman who rescued me from Cotton Street and sent that message through. How she's mixed up in the business I don't know, but she seems to be pretty well acquainted with Brandt's movements. There is just a chance that she may know where he is.'

'A lot of help that's going to be to us,' snorted Shadgold.

'What I'm driving at,' said Lowe impatiently, 'is this. If she let us know once where to find Al Brandt, it is by no means impossible that she'll do so a second time.'

Shadgold shrugged his shoulders sceptically. 'We can't count on it,' he muttered.

'You can't count on anything,' retorted the dramatist. 'Brandt's clever, and unless

I'm very much mistaken, he won't try to leave the country by any of the ordinary methods; in which case, all the police in the world keeping a lookout for him won't catch him.'

'All the same,' said Shadgold, 'it's no good depending on miracles.'

'Except,' broke in Lowe, 'they happen more often than people imagine.'

White, who had been sitting on the edge of the desk silently looking at the floor, suddenly looked up. 'You said just now, Mr. Lowe,' he remarked, 'that Brandt wouldn't attempt to leave the country by any of the ordinary methods.'

'Well?' Lowe looked at the secretary expectantly.

'Well, there is one way he might try,' went on White quickly. 'There are any number of cargo boats whose captains will agree to take a passenger for a small consideration: fruit boats, currant boats and the like.'

'That's an idea,' said Trevor Lowe. 'In which case, of course, he'd go downriver. The majority of such boats leave from points near the mouth of the Thames.' He

turned to Shadgold. 'S'pose you get . . . '
he began, and was interrupted by the
shrill summons of the telephone.

Shadgold pulled the instrument towards
him and lifted the receiver. 'Hello!' he
barked, and after a pause: 'Headin' downriver, you say? Right! See if you can pick
up any further traces.' He banged the
black cylinder on its hook and swung round
towards Lowe. 'That was from the Wap-
ping division of the Thames Police. They've
got hold of a lighterman who reports having
seen a launch without lights headin' downstream at a little after three. It's ten to one
that's our man.'

'Yes, and it bears out White's theory,'
said the dramatist. 'He was probably making
for Gravesend, or some similar place.'

'I've told T.P. to report at once if they
get any further news,' said the Scotland
Yard man. 'It's no good going off on a
wild goose chase until we can get some
sort of an idea where we are making for.'

'No,' said Lowe. 'There are any number
of places where he may have put in after
he was seen by the lighterman.'

Shadgold had opened his mouth to

reply when there came a tap at the door and a uniformed constable came in. He laid an oblong envelope on the desk in front of the inspector. 'Just come, sir,' he announced, 'by special messenger.'

Shadgold ripped it open, glanced at the single sheet of paper that it contained, and raised his eyebrows. 'That clears up one thing at any rate,' he said, and tossed it over to Lowe. It was a cablegram from New York and read:

'Police message. Very urgent. Clear the line.

'To Detective-Inspector Shadgold,
'New Scotland Yard,
'London, England.
'Message begins:
'Answer your enquiry D.1306. Al Brandt, head of the Boxer Gang, Chicago, disappeared after the shooting of Michael Ahearn. Kit Ahearn, the dead man's wife, also disappeared the same time. Believed to have followed Brandt. Known to have uttered threats against him. Description: tall, slim, blue eyes, age thirty-five, complexion fair, hair dark. No trace of

304

Brandt or the woman since come to hand. Message ends.'

Lowe read the message twice, and then laid it down. 'That, I think, explains the woman,' he said. 'It has puzzled me a great deal to know who she was, and how she became mixed up in this business, but this message seems to clear that up. The description tallies with the woman of Cotton Street.'

'And we know why she's been sticking so tight to Al Brandt,' grunted the inspector. He stretched out his hand and pressed the bell on his desk. 'Might as well have some coffee while we're waiting,' he suggested, and when the messenger arrived in answer to his summons he gave a brief order.

When it came, they drank the hot coffee gratefully while they waited as patiently as they could for further news of the fugitive. It was over an hour before they heard anything, and then another telephone call came through. The captain of a barge had seen a motorboat answering the description supplied by the lighterman going downriver in the direction of Gravesend. It was about three miles from Gravesend where he had seen it.

'Gravesend is where he is making for,' said Lowe. 'There is very little doubt of that. You had better notify the Gravesend police to be on the lookout.'

Shadgold rang up the clerk in charge of the switchboard and asked to be put through. Some little time elapsed before the connection was established, and then he was speaking to the sergeant-in-charge at the Gravesend police station. He gave a brief description of Al Brandt and the launch, and asked that all patrols should be warned to look out for the man. His message, as it happened, was a little late, for at the time the sergeant at Gravesend received it, Al Brandt was already sleeping peacefully in his bedroom at the obscure little hotel.

Another hour dragged by, and the pale yellow gleam of the morning sun was slanting in through the window of the inspector's office when the telephone rang again. At the first sound of the voice that came over the wire, Shadgold almost dropped the receiver.

'Yes, he's here,' he said. 'Just a moment.' Holding his hand over the mouthpiece, he turned excitedly to Lowe. 'Somebody wants to speak to you,' he said. 'A woman.'

The dramatist reached over for the instrument and put the receiver to his ear. 'Hello!' he called softly. 'This is Trevor Lowe speaking.'

A low, rather musical voice answered him, and he recognised it instantly. It was the lady of Cotton Street! 'I've been trying your house, Mr. Lowe,' she said. 'But I couldn't get any reply, so I got on to Scotland Yard on the off-chance that you might be there.'

'And you were right, Mrs. Ahearn,' said the dramatist.

He heard a little exclamation at the other end of the wire. 'So you know who I am?' she said. 'Well, I don't know that it matters much. I've just rung up to tell you where you can find Al Brandt. He is at a small hotel in Gravesend, the Sailors' Rest. It's in a narrow turning off the main street; you can't mistake it.' There was a click as she hung up the receiver, and Trevor Lowe laid down the telephone and sprang to his feet.

'Phone the Gravesend police, Shadgold,' he said, 'and tell them to go at once to the Sailors' Rest.' He repeated the message he had received. 'You had better order a fast car at once,' he added.

The burly inspector carried out both suggestions with alacrity. Ten minutes later they were speeding through the fresh morning air in a police tender en route for Gravesend.

30

The Lady of Doom

The woman who had arrived in a mud-spattered car in the early hours of the morning entered the dingy portals of the Sailors' Rest, and to the astonished man behind the reception desk asked if she could be supplied with some coffee.

'I think so, madam,' he stammered, for he was not used to receiving women in that establishment. 'If you will go into the coffee-room I'll send a waiter to you.'

Kit Ahearn thanked him and made her way into the cheerless room with its long, white-clothed table. She seated herself by the big fireplace in which the remains of the previous day's fire — a heap of blackened cinders and white ash — still lingered in the grate. Although outwardly calm, her heart was beating fast.

The moment for which she had waited was close at hand, here under the same roof as the man she hated — the man whom she had followed for so long. She felt in her handbag to assure herself that the things she would need were there.

The elderly waiter came bustling in to take her order, and when he returned with the tray of coffee she gently detained him. 'I think you have a friend of mine staying with you,' she said hesitantly. 'He arrived early this morning. I was to meet him here.'

The waiter nodded. 'Yes, madam,' he answered. 'That would be the gentleman in Room 10. He is the only person who arrived this morning. Very tired he was, too. Shall I tell him you're here? He's asleep now.'

She shook her head quickly. 'No, no, don't disturb him,' she said. 'I got here before I expected to. I'll wait.'

The elderly waiter, who scented romance, bowed, and was on the point of withdrawing when she called him back.

'If,' she said, 'there was somewhere where I could wash . . . ?' She looked at him enquiringly.

'I'll ask,' he said, and hurried away.

After the lapse of a few seconds he returned holding a key. 'If you will come with me,' he said, and waited while she drank the coffee which was poured out.

She rose and he led the way out of the coffee-room and up a flight of stairs covered with carpet that the tramp of many feet had worn threadbare. They reached a narrow corridor, and halfway along this he paused and opened a door with the key he carried, ushering her into a small sparsely furnished bedroom. 'If you will wait here for a minute or two,' he said, 'I'll bring you some hot water.'

She thanked him, and, taking off the heavy coat she wore, sat down on the side of the bed. As she had expected and hoped, he had left the key in the lock. She waited, sitting motionless until the water had been brought and the waiter had again taken his departure. Then, peering out into the corridor to make certain there was no one about to observe her movements, she withdrew the key from the lock and tiptoed softly in the direction of the staircase.

Her quick eyes had noted the door of Number 10 when they had passed it on their way to the room where she had been taken to wash. Now, pausing outside the closed door, she listened. The sound of faint breathing came to her from inside the room, and with infinite caution she stooped and inserted the key she had taken from the door of the other room in the lock. But it refused to go fully in, and a moment's thought told her the reason why. The other key, turned from inside, prevented it.

Swiftly she returned to the room where she had left her handbag, and, picking it up, rapidly searched through its contents. She found what she wanted, and made her way back again along the corridor to the closed door of Number 10.

For a few seconds she worked on the lock with the piece of stiff wire which she had brought back with her, and presently had the satisfaction of hearing the key fall with a sharp thud on to the floor inside. She listened to hear if the sound had awakened the sleeper, but the steady breathing went on unabated. Now she once more placed the other key in the lock, and this time it slipped in easily. Softly she turned it, and with a gentle click the catch slid back. She tried the handle and found that the door opened easily, but she made no attempt as yet to enter the room.

Instead, she hurried back to her own apartment and put her coat on. Taking something from her handbag, she dropped it into her pocket, stuffed the bag itself into the other pocket, closed and locked the door of the room, and went back to Number 10.

For a moment she stood, her hand on the handle. Then, a figure of Nemesis, she opened the door and entered the room where Al Brandt lay sleeping. She shut the door behind her, picked up the key from the floor, and locked it, and then crossed over to the bed.

With her lips compressed into a hard line, she stood looking down at the sleeping man. Then, bending forward, she touched him on the shoulder. 'Wake up!' she said.

He grunted, opened his eyes, and stared blearily at the figure standing over him; stared also at the pistol, with its silencer clamped to the barrel, which she held in her right hand. Then recognising who it was, he started up, supporting himself on one elbow.

'Keep still,' said Kit Ahearn. 'Don't move!'

He crouched back, his face grey with fear. There was no mistaking that voice — the voice he had been dreading to hear for two years, the voice that had haunted his dreams and many of his waking hours, the voice that on a rainy night in Chicago had cried: 'No matter where you go or where you hide, I'll get you!'

'Kit!' he gasped; and again: 'Kit!'

The figure of the woman towered above him, and, without removing her eyes from his — those hard eyes which seemed to burn into his brain — she nodded.

'Yes, Kit,' she answered. 'I've always been pretty close to you, Al. I had a flat in the same building. For two years I've followed you like a shadow, and for two years I've waited for this moment — to get you in the hour of your triumph.'

The terror-stricken man licked his parched lips. 'Let's not quarrel, Kit,' he whispered. 'I'll do anything I can. I'll do anything you ask. You can have money — lots of money.

I'll give you anything — everything. Only, have mercy!'

She laughed a low, bitter, mirthless laugh. 'Ask Dan and Ike for mercy,' she said. 'Ask Jim Cornish for mercy. Ask Mike for mercy. They are more likely to hear you than I. If you know a prayer, say it, for it's the last thing you'll say on this earth.'

She raised the hand that held the pistol, and Al Brandt, seeing her finger whiten on the trigger, knew that his doom was at hand. Desperately he flung out a hand in a frantic attempt to grasp that menacing muzzle. There was a flash of orange flame and a dull *plop*. For a second he fell back, clawing the air; and then his hands dropped, and he lay an inert thing of lifeless clay.

★   ★   ★

The big police car rushed on, reeling the miles out behind it. Shadgold had taken the precaution before leaving the Yard to have the road cleared for them, so that there would be no trouble with speed

315

regulations and hold-ups. The inspector himself occupied the seat beside the driver, with Lowe and White in the back. They spoke very little, for each one's thoughts were occupied with what lay ahead. The sun was well up when they came into Gravesend and drew up with a jerk before the narrow portal of the Sailors' Rest.

The first thing they saw as they got out of the car was the burly figure of a uniformed policeman standing just inside the entrance. The man came forward as they crossed the intervening strip of pavement, and saluted Shadgold when the latter made known his identity. 'The inspector's upstairs, sir,' he said, jerking his thumb towards the inside of the hotel. 'Pretty bad business too.'

'Pretty bad business!' snapped Shadgold. 'What's a pretty bad business?'

'This 'ere murder, sir,' said the constable.

'Murder?' said Lowe quickly. 'Who's been killed?' He asked the question, but subconsciously he knew before the man had time to reply.

'The feller you telephoned about,' said the constable. 'We came round here from the station according to instructions, and found that a man answering to your description had come in early this morning and booked a room. The manager said he was sleeping, and we went upstairs and knocked on the door to wake him up, but we couldn't get no reply, and we thought at first he had bolted. When we broke in the door, however, we found him all right. Stone dead he was — shot through the chest.'

The policeman stopped with evident relish, and was going on adding some gruesome details when Shadgold checked his morbid flow of speech. 'Take us up to your inspector at once,' he said shortly.

The constable led the way up the dingy staircase and along a corridor towards the open door of a room on the left. A tall uniformed man was standing just inside the doorway talking to a shorter and stouter individual in plain clothes. He swung round as the newcomers paused on the threshold, and frowned.

'What are these people doing here,

Halkit?' he snapped. 'I thought I told you to see — ' The constable ventured an explanation, and the local inspector's face cleared. 'Oh, you're Inspector Shadgold, are you?' he said, addressing the Scotland Yard man. 'Well, we seem to have arrived too late here. Somebody else was before us, and your man's been killed.' He nodded towards the bed on which a still and silent figure lay.

'Any idea who did it?' asked Shadgold.

The local man nodded. 'Oh, yes!' he answered. 'There's no doubt at all who did it. It was a woman who came here this morning and said she was a friend of the dead man's. She said she had an appointment to meet him here, but if he was asleep she didn't want him disturbed.'

'Kit Ahearn!' exclaimed Shadgold.

'Ahearn, did you say?' said the inspector. 'Yes, that was the name on the paper.'

'Paper? What paper?' asked Lowe.

'The paper we found on the body,' replied the inspector. 'It was pinned to the sheet. It's still there; you can see it for yourselves.' He led the way over to the bed and pointed down to half a sheet of notepaper that was pinned to the coverlet. On it was a pencilled scrawl, and Trevor Lowe's face set as he read the wording:

'In memory of Mike Ahearn.'

'Kit Ahearn evidently kept her word,' he said, and looked across at Shadgold.

★ ★ ★

'I hope you don't get her,' said Gregory Carr, lounging in a chair in Lowe's study in Portland Place. It was two days later, and he had called round to see the dramatist, and had learned of the fate that had overtaken Al Brandt. 'I, for one, hope she gets away. She did the world a service when she shot that brute.'

'I'm inclined to agree with you,' said Trevor Lowe. 'And in spite of the fact that the Yard have notified the stations and patrols to look for her, I somehow don't think they'll find the lady.' He blew out a cloud of smoke. 'She played fair, after all. She gave us the chance of getting Brandt, and when we lost him she stepped in. I hope she gets away with it.'

She did get away with it, for, from the

morning when she had walked quietly out of the Sailors' Rest after settling her debt with Brandt, Kit Ahearn disappeared for good. The sad-faced lady who lives a secluded life in the sun-drenched villa facing the sea beyond Monaco is known by quite a different name.

There was a slight pause, and then Gregory put the question that had been the reason for his calling, and which had been hovering on the tip of his tongue for some considerable time. 'Have you seen anything of — ' he began hesitantly.

Lowe finished the sentence for him. 'The woman?' he asked with a twinkle in his eyes. 'Yes, I had a long talk with her yesterday. I'm sorry for her, poor little thing. She was fond of that brother of hers, though from all accounts he was a bit of a waster. She did her best to get him away from the influence of Brandt. When she found out he was in his clutches, she followed her brother over and over again to try and save him from getting deeper into the mire. She was afraid to seek help from the police for fear her brother would be arrested, too. She's got pluck, I must say that.'

'Of course she's got pluck,' said Gregory. Reddening, he went on: 'By the way, do you know where she's living at the moment? She's moved from that flat in Alerdyce Road. I went round there yesterday, and they told me — '

'She's staying with some friends,' said the dramatist. 'Nineteen, Elm Park Gardens. It's a turning off Kensington High Street. I think the flat was associated too much in her mind with the trouble over her brother. Are you going?' he asked innocently, as Gregory rose to his feet.

'Yes — er — I've just remembered an important appointment,' mumbled Gregory incoherently. 'I'll drop in again some other time. Goodbye!'

'Goodbye!' said Trevor Lowe. 'By the way, Ann Cornish is rather a pretty name, don't you think?'

'Yes, very,' said Gregory from the doorway. 'Why?'

'Only that it seems rather a pity to ask her to change it,' said the dramatist, but the slamming of the door was his only reply.

We do hope that you have enjoyed reading this large print book.

Did you know that all of our titles are available for purchase?

We publish a wide range of high quality large print books including:

Romances, Mysteries, Classics
General Fiction
Non Fiction and Westerns

Special interest titles available in large print are:

The Little Oxford Dictionary
Music Book, Song Book
Hymn Book, Service Book

Also available from us courtesy of Oxford University Press:

Young Readers' Dictionary
(large print edition)
Young Readers' Thesaurus
(large print edition)

For further information or a free brochure, please contact us at:
Ulverscroft Large Print Books Ltd.,
The Green, Bradgate Road, Anstey,
Leicester, LE7 7FU, England.
Tel: (00 44) **0116 236 4325**
Fax: (00 44) **0116 234 0205**

DARK JOURNEY

Catriona McCuaig

Midwife Maudie Bryant is used to stumbling across murder — but now that she is the mother of a little boy, she has vowed to leave any future crime-solving to her husband Dick, a policeman. However, death strikes too close to home when a wealthy local woman, Cora Beasley, is found strangled with a belt from Maudie's dress. To make matters worse, it is well known that Maudie believed 'the beastly woman was out to snare Dick'. Can Detective Sergeant Bryant help to solve the crime before Maudie is charged as a suspect?

SHERLOCK HOLMES VS. FRANKENSTEIN

David Whitehead

An intriguing mystery lures Sherlock Holmes from the comfort of Baker Street in the winter of 1898: the ghastly murder of a gravedigger in the most bizarre of circumstances. Soon Holmes and Watson are travelling to the tiny German village of Darmstadt, to unmask a callous killer with an even more terrifying motive . . . In nearby Schloss Frankenstein, the eponymous family disowns the rumours attached to its infamous ancestor. But the past cannot be erased, and an old evil is growing strong once again — in the unlikeliest of guises . . .

THE RADIO RED KILLER

Richard A. Lupoff

Veteran broadcaster 'Radio Red' Bob Bjorner is the last of the red-hot lefties working at radio station KRED in Berkeley. His paranoia makes him lock his studio against intruders while he's on the air — but his precaution doesn't save him from a horrible death that leaves him slumped at the microphone just before his three o'clock daily broadcast. Homicide detective Marvia Plum scrambles to the station to investigate. Who amongst the broadcasters, engineers, and administrators present at the station was the murderer — and why?

THE BIG FELLOW

Gerald Verner and Chris Verner

Young Inspector Jim Holland of Scotland Yard is under particular pressure to bring to justice 'The Big Fellow' — the mastermind behind a gang committing ever more audacious outrages. As the newspapers mount virulent attacks on Scotland Yard for failing to deal with the rogues, and the crimes escalate from robbery to brutal murder, Holland finds not only his own life threatened, but also that of his theatre actress girlfriend, Diana Carrington.

Also included is the story, *The Man on the Train*.

BLING-BLING, YOU'RE DEAD!

Geraldine Ryan

When the manager of newly-formed girl band Bling-Bling needs a Surveillance Operator to protect them, retired policeman Bill Muir jumps at the chance — but he doesn't know what he's let himself in for . . . In *Making Changes*, Tania Harkness is on a mission to turn around her run-down estate. But someone else is equally determined to stop her . . . And in *Another Country*, Shona Graham returns to her native Orkney island of Hundsay to put right a wrong that saw her brother ostracised by the community many years perviously . . .

THE DOPPELGÄNGER DEATHS

Edmund Glasby

While investigating a fatal car crash, Detective Inspector Vaughn's interest is piqued when forensic evidence points to murder, and he is shown the eerie antique doll found sitting on the passenger seat. The blood-spattered doll bears an extraordinary resemblance to the dead man, and on its lap is an envelope containing the message: 'One down. Five to go.' When a second doll is discovered beside another murder victim, the desperate race is then on to find and stop the killer from completing the set of six murders . . .